DEATH'S FOOTPRINT

Book 2 in a Blair and Piermont crime thriller series

DONNA WARNER
GLORIA FERRIS

GENRE: MYSTERY/CRIME THRILLER/QUICK READ

DEATH'S FOOTPRINT

Copyright @ 2016 by Donna Warner & Gloria Ferris

Cover Design: Cheryl R. Cowtan

All cover art from CanStock.ca 2017

Electronic ISBN: 978-0-9952248-1-0

Print ISBN: 978-0-9952248-0-3

First Publication: APRIL 2017

Library and Archives Canada Cataloguing in Publication

NOTE TO READERS

DEATH'S FOOTPRINT is SET IN OLD QUÉBEC CITY, CANADA. THE CITY is hundreds of years older than Canadian Confederation (1867). The historic stone architecture and narrow, winding streets make visitors feel they have been transported to a romantic European city.

A few scenes take place in the spectacular Fairmont Château Frontenac, the castle-like hotel overlooking the St. Lawrence River. We stayed there during our research trip, and it was truly an experience we'll never forget.

Signage in Québec City is in French, including street names, so a heads-up to readers who may wonder at the references to "rue des Jardins", or "rue des Parlementaires". We also retained the accents on French words.

Merci, and happy reading!

Donna Warner

Gloria Ferris

CHAPTER ONE

Tuesday, 9:00 a.m.

BEHIND HIS BACK, THEY CALLED HIM DR. DEATH. THE NICKNAME secretly delighted Professor Lucas Stride. He thrived on nurturing young minds, and this lot had been a joy to teach, with one exception.

Lucas toggled the light switch by the lecture room door. This silenced the fifteen students, some chattering like howler monkeys in heat.

After thirty-eight years of teaching, projecting his voice to the back of the room was effortless. "Since this is our final classroom session, I want to share a quote from Ralph Waldo Emerson that sums up this course's mission statement."

The professor adjusted his wire-framed glasses before reciting from the page in his hand: *"The purpose of life is to be useful, to be honorable, to be compassionate, to have it make some difference that you have lived and lived well."*

"In other words, leave a memorable footprint." He paused to allow his students to digest the words.

"I hope you've found our discussions enlightening. Thanks for taking

1

the *Death's Reality* course instead of spending your summer binge drinking at a beach."

Polite snickers and one heckle acknowledged his words. "Next week, your grade and course certificate will be mailed to you. With field trips to the Orsainville Detention Centre, a hospice home, a funeral parlour, and a cemetery behind us, any idea where our final excursion will take us?"

An arm shot up above the heart-shaped face of a young woman in the front row. When he stared at her, hesitating to invite her answer, her smile broadened as if encouraging him to take his time remembering her name.

Finally, a couple of phantom neurons fired. "Kelsi. Your guess is?"

"Are we going to the cancer treatment centre at Hôtel-Dieu de Québec?"

A male student, slightly older than the others, leaned over and whispered to the blonde woman beside him. She frowned and slapped his arm before moving three seats over. Satisfied that his comment provoked a response, he smirked.

Lucas had overlooked this student's rude disruptions on many occasions over the past five weeks. Not today.

"Jared Kavello. Do you have something you wish to share with the rest of us?"

"Why so formal, Professor? As I've told you repeatedly, call me Jag. Are you going to try and shock us by looking at corpses in a morgue?"

The professor forced a smile. "Very insightful of you, Jared." This was one student he wouldn't miss when the summer course at Université Laval concluded on Friday.

He broke eye contact with Jared and addressed the rest of the class. "Dr. Aurore Colet, Québec City's medical examiner, will discuss how the deceased are processed and what is involved in an autopsy. For those of you who choose a career path in health care, gaining insight into coping with dying patients and making final arrangements for the body are paramount."

there will be a tour of the body storage area. It isn't mandatory you attend, and I won't embarrass you by asking for a show of hands. Fill out the form on your desk if you'll be joining us and hand it to me along with the course evaluation sheet before you leave. We'll meet in the parking lot of the morgue on Blvd. Wilfrid Hamel at 4:30 p.m. on Friday.

Looking directly at Jared, he said, "And I don't need to remind you that a respectful decorum is required while in the morgue."

This earned him a brazen stare from Jared, along with a mouthed comment that the deaf would translate as, "Whatever you say, old man." After decades in the classroom, the professor was a proficient lip reader.

"That's it for today people."

As the students bowed their heads to the assigned task, Lucas added, "One more thing. I urge you to skip lunch on Friday. Formaldehyde can be unsettling to one's stomach."

Gathering his belongings, he leaned against the door frame at the back of the room, and waited to collect the completed sheets.

Once the students left, he tallied the consent forms. Only fourteen.

CHAPTER TWO

Tuesday, 10:00 a.m.

DARCY PIERMONT SCOWLED AT THE ROLEX ON HIS NIGHT STAND. THE watch had been a gift from his mother last year for his twenty-ninth birthday. Shit, he'd better get his ass moving. Rolling out of bed, he offered a prayer to the god of hiring lotteries that today would produce a winner.

He opened his underwear drawer and sorted through the eclectic collection to find something that matched his mood. He discarded trunks, thongs, and boxers, choosing a pair of purple low-rise briefs.

A second drawer stowed an assortment of T-shirts, with and without slogans. Nope. Today's interview required a more professional look. From his closet, he scooped up a dress shirt, jeans, and leather sandals and headed to the bathroom.

Darcy showered and shaved quickly, only slowing down to avoid injuring the slight cleft in his chin. A slap of gel to make his blond mini-Mohawk stand at attention, and he was good to go.

He felt fortunate to have scored a townhouse on rue des Jardins, in the trendy Upper Town area of Old Québec City. He was behind schedule in the unpacking department, but *c'est la vie*.

About to walk past the mountain of packing boxes, he remembered that tonight there better be sheets on the bed. He eyed the sleeping bag he'd been using for the past week. That wouldn't do for Jordan. Spying a box with the word "Bedroom" scrawled on the side, he tossed it on the bed and slit the cello tape with a utility knife from his dresser.

Dieu merci! Sheets. Which set would she like? White cotton, black silk, red satin? He went with the black silk and skillfully made up the bed, finishing off with a white duvet. He wiped a thin layer of dust from the night tables and dressers with the damp towel from his shower. Done.

His stomach grumbled as he took the stairs down, two at a time. Whether the complaint was due to its empty condition or last night's Scotch tasting with a friend he once worked with in Border Services, was anyone's guess.

He took a hurried slurp of his coffee en route to the office. Dropping into the chair, he speed-read the résumé of today's applicant.

Five minutes later, his doorbell chimed the opening bars of Beethoven's Symphony No. 5. He snickered, and thought he might install a camera on the front steps to capture the expression on visitors' faces as they considered which of the three white and two black piano keys to press.

He opened the oak door. There stood a young woman studying the brass plaque on the wall above the bell: *Enquêtes Piermont*.

"Piermont Investigations. I'm at the right place," she remarked, eyes travelling from the plaque to the piano keys, then up to his face. "Darcy Piermont, I presume. The first door I knocked on belonged to a cranky old dude who said he didn't want to buy any Girl Scout cookies. He slammed the door in my face."

She reached out and clasped his hand in a firm shake. "Kelsi Chong."

"Delighted, Miss Chong. I can't say I've had the pleasure of meeting any of my neighbours yet. Something to look forward to, I'm sure. Don't fret. Thirty years from now, you'll pay someone to mistake you for a preteen. But, I digress. Yes, you've found me. Not sure if that will make your day better or worse."

"I guess we'll see how this interview goes, Mr. Piermont. I'm pumped to dazzle you with my knowledge of your business."

"Splendid. In that case, do come in."

The last two interviews had been a bust, and this one could be headed down the same thorny path. Guiding her past the reception area to his office, he marvelled at how Miss Chong could walk gracefully in boots with four-inch stiletto heels. Without them, she'd be five foot nothing.

"Please make yourself comfortable." Darcy motioned to the leather couch in the sitting area of his office. He sat in the arm chair across from her. Miss Chong gave her short skirt a tug after her bottom touched down.

She eyed the stacks of paper on his desk. "Man, I can see why you need help. Quite a mess you have here." She shook her head and uttered a soft chiding sound. Her red lipstick made a striking contrast with her almond complexion.

"You aren't afraid of speaking your mind, are you, Miss Chong? I like that."

"Nope. And you can call me Kelsi."

A few stubborn strands of charcoal-colored hair escaped from her up-do. She pushed them back behind her left ear and lowered her designer tote to the rug.

Giving his office the once over, she said, "Nice place you have here, Mr. P. After hoofing it from the bus stop, my throat is as dry as beach sand. Is it too early for a glass of chardonnay?"

Darcy didn't need to consult his watch. "I believe it is. How about joining me for a cup of coffee instead?"

"I guess. Black with two sugars, if you don't mind."

"Fine, then. Be right back."

In the kitchen, Darcy shook his head. Had he already lost control of the interview? He brought their cups back and set them on the teak table.

Kelsi said, "Ah, thanks, Mr. P." Her first sip was tentative, followed by a slight gulp.

Darcy collected Kelsi's résumé from his desk. "I see you're bilingual. Excellent." Applicants one and two had run for the door after this question was posed to them.

"*Comment bien parlez-vous français?*" He waited for her reaction.

"*Je parle français Parisien et le français du Québec.*"

Darcy blinked and swung into English. "You speak Parisian French and Québec French. Where did you learn to speak Parisian?"

Kelsi took a prolonged sip from her cup. "I have a French-speaking grandmother on my mother's side. I spent summers with her in Provence when I was a kid."

"*Très bien.* That's one prerequisite out of the way."

Darcy wrote a note on her résumé, looking up to catch her giving the dolphin tattoo on his left forearm the once-over. "This is the head office for Piermont Private Investigations."

"That's why I applied for the job." She placed her empty cup down and crossed her short, shapely legs.

"Oh? We have branch offices in London, England and in Madrid, Spain. Our head office was in Montréal until I moved it here last week."

"Yes, I know about your other offices. Your mother is the CEO and operates from Madrid. One of your uncles runs the London office. Your father was British and your mother is Québécois. I checked you out online."

"Of course you did. So, where was I? Oh yes. I see from your cover letter that you are enrolled in a distance education course at Humber College in Toronto. You have one more semester to complete to earn your Protection, Security and Investigations Diploma. Correct?"

"*Oui*, Mr. P."

Darcy winced at her responsive rhyme. "That's an unexpected plus. Will it be a problem for you to work full-time while completing your course work?"

"Of course not. I'm a woman, hear me roar." Her impish smile showcased flawless, white teeth.

Darcy dropped his pen. After bending to retrieve it, he noticed Kelsi examining his hair.

"Nice junior Mohawk you have going," she said.

"Thanks. Now, how are your bookkeeping skills?"

"I not only manage my finances, I pay my *grand-père* and *grand-mère's* bills since they're in their late 70s."

"That's commendable but will you be able to persuade clients with accounts in arrears to pay up?"

"I can be highly persuasive, Mr. P. With an Irish mother and a Chinese father, I can be as solemn as a mourner at a wake or spout dragon flames from my tongue."

After Darcy digested that image, he reactivated his own tongue. "Jolly good, then. According to your résumé, you're proficient with Microsoft Word and Excel." He resisted the notion of testing her skills in this area. No doubt, she was as capable as she claimed.

They went over the hours of work and salary. "Are you still interested in this position?"

"Most definitely," Kelsi replied, without hesitation.

"Any questions for me?"

"Just one. After I get my diploma, can I do some wet work with you?"

Darcy hesitated before responding. "I hope you mean field work. I hate to disillusion you, but the services I provide lean towards surveilling unfaithful partners, investigating fraud and embezzlement, and contract work from crown attorneys."

"Well, maybe things will jazz up when I'm here, "she said with a twenty-two year old's optimism. "In the meantime, I'm fine with assignments that will launch my ass out of a chair from time to time."

"Let's see how you do with this pile of paperwork first. When are you available to start?"

"I thought I already did."

"In that case, follow me to your work station. Please greet walk-in clients and phone enquiries in French and English and screen calls prior to transferring them to me. Our operatives will call my cell number, so you shouldn't have to deal with them."

"You got it."

"Kick back while I make a call. You can fill out the employment paperwork you'll find on your desk. I'll join you in a few minutes and give you the password to your computer. And Kelsi, I have a friend flying in today from Toronto, so don't schedule any appointments until next Monday. You can reach me on my cell if any urgent matters crop up. By the way, my living quarters are upstairs." Darcy nodded toward the hall and the winding oak staircase.

"Is your friend a woman?"

"*Oui*. Most definitely."

"Is she staying here with you?"

"*Oui*."

"Hope there's lots of insulation in the walls."

Darcy swallowed. "No worries. I had a state-of-the-art stereo system installed. The controls are behind the panel beside the window. You can always punch up the volume."

"Way to plan ahead, boss."

"Please call me Darcy unless we have a client and then make it Monsieur or Mister Piermont."

"It's a deal, boss. I mean, Darcy. I have one field-trip left in my university summer course. Would it be a problem if I left at 3:30 p.m. Friday? I'll stay late Thursday night."

"Not necessary. The answering machine can pick up calls that afternoon."

What would Jordan make of his new hire? God help him if he'd made a holy shit mistake.

CHAPTER THREE

Tuesday, 11:00 a.m.

JAG KAVELLO GLANCED AT THE WOMAN SEATED BESIDE HIM ON THE bench in front of his student residence building. She droned on about her career aspirations, her voice lulling him into a coma-like state.

A couple of months ago, things got too hot in Ottawa. He had been forced to stash his belongings, including a 2013 Jaguar XJ Supersport, in a storage facility. The Jaguar was a magnet for cops. He couldn't take the chance of being pulled over. Leasing a gutless grey Taurus for his weeks in Québec City seemed safer.

Sure, he loved fast cars, party girls, and easy money deals. So what?

He was determined to make up for a childhood spent in the Calgary foster care system. He had problems making friends in his new neighbourhoods, and resorted to bragging that he invented the contraptions on the Red Green television series. When that didn't fly, he would grab his genitals and imitate Michael Jackson's pre-pubescent voice on the *Thriller* video. This, at least, earned him some squeals of laughter from younger boys. Performing — and lying — came naturally to him.

Jag smirked as he remembered other talents surfacing during stints with various foster parents. He was forced to leave his first placement when they noticed money disappearing from their wallets. He was too much of an amateur back then to simply deny it.

He managed to charm the Edwards, foster parents number four — or was it five? They remained ignorant of his ability to play them and, thanks to their benevolent neglect, he had the freedom to become a street entrepreneur at age 14, working as a drug mule. No one ever suspected him. The job gave him the financial independence to leave the Edwards and the street gang and strike out on his own two years later.

Jag received a high school equivalency diploma by correspondence and was accepted into the Bachelor of Business Administration program at Mount Royal University. With his degree in hand and an acumen in finance and marketing, he set his sights on selling financial packages to losers who couldn't manage their own money. He set up his office in Ottawa four years ago.

A sharp elbow to his ribs jolted him out of the past and reminded him to focus on the woman beside him.

His fingers slipped from her shoulder to caress the top of her left breast. "So, Sherryn, you're very friendly with our professor. Are you banging him to get a better grade?"

Sherryn shoved his arm away. "Don't be gross. He's close to my grandfather's age. I feel bad that he recently lost his wife. Besides, he's a good teacher. This Philosophy course will complement my B.A. in Gerontology. I'm applying for positions in health care management when I go home."

"You're such a softy. I'm sure a career of holding old farts' hands will be a good fit for you." He leaned over to plant a kiss on her ear.

Sherryn jerked her face away so his lips skidded off her cheekbone.

"Easy now, baby. Just kidding about you being teacher's pet. Personally, I've had my fill of Dr. Death's bullshit preaching. Acting like a Mother Theresa so people have good thoughts about us when we kick the bucket? Not happening. When the Grim Reaper comes for me, I plan to tell him to fuck off, then run over him in my sports car."

Sherryn threw him a look out of the corner of her eye. "Your social conscience is totally non-existent. And I've asked you not to call me baby." She shot up from the bench and headed towards her car.

He caught up with her, this time keeping his hands to himself. "Don't be pissed with me. I'll take you out for dinner. You choose the place. Call me this afternoon and tell me where you want to meet up."

Noticing the set of her lips, he fished for another enticement. "You've been telling me how tight your finances are lately. I've got a money-making proposition to discuss with you."

"You do?" Sherryn said with a mild display of interest. "My kitchen utensils are packed up, so it would be good to eat out. I'm all ears if you have tips on how I can get my debts paid. But, you have to lay off trash talking Professor Stride."

Jag raised his hands in surrender while hiding his satisfaction. "It's a deal."

He'd better watch his mouth, or the plans he had for this bitch would go up in smoke.

CHAPTER FOUR

Tuesday, 12:30 p.m.

RECALLING THE CRACKHEAD WHO SPIT ON HER SHIRT LAST NIGHT, Jordan plunged the knife into a block of cheese on her kitchenette counter. Her phone rang, and she dashed into the compact room she referred to as her study with sandwich in hand. A couple of recliners, a wall-mounted television, and two side tables comprised the living space of her condo in The Beaches area of Toronto.

"Damn it, where did I leave my phone?" she muttered. The ringing originated from one of the recliners, and she slid her fingers under the cushion. Got it!

"Yeah?"

"Good afternoon, luv. How's my warrior princess today?"

"Tired but hanging in. Last night was my tenth shift. And, feel free to call me Constable Blair," Jordan responded. "Failing that, warrior queen will do." She laughed. "You're never going to let me live down what I had to do to that dickhead in Honduras who tried to kidnap me and Ellie, are you?"

"Never going to happen. I fantasize regularly over seeing you in combat stance, at the side of a mountain road with your hair messed up, face smudged with dirt, and a dagger clutched in your hand."

Jordan snorted. "Well, a girl's got to use whatever weapon is handy to defend herself."

"Exactly. I believe I may need to see more action during your visit to boost my fantasy collection."

"I'll see what I can do." Jordan shook off a flush of excitement, imagining the possibilities.

After they parted at the Honduran airport last spring, Darcy pursued her relentlessly via e-mails and phone calls, finally convincing her that he was worth getting to know.

The weekend he spent with her in Toronto a few months ago had torqued their relationship up several notches. Still, she intended to tread cautiously down the romance path with this man whose personality pendulum swung between exasperating and irresistibly sexy.

"Am I catching you at a bad time? I'm confirming that you'll be on this afternoon's flight."

Jordan bit into her sandwich and talked through a mouthful. "Count on it. As soon as we hang up, I'm turning off my phone so my sergeant can't call me in at the last minute. I'm leaving for the airport in half an hour."

"If you're naked, can I coax you into setting your iPhone on FaceTime?"

"Negative, you horny Francophone. I'm looking forward to five days with you at your new place, treading the cobblestoned streets of Old Québec. Immersing myself in 400 years of history is as high on my list as testing your bedsprings."

"Spoil sport about the FaceTime. However, my sweet, I promise to fulfill your every desire. At night, we'll dine at the finest pubs and drink wine that tastes like angel spit."

Jordan flinched at the spit word. "Don't go to any trouble for me," she told him, knowing the restaurants and wine Darcy chose would render her forever dissatisfied with her usual Toronto pubs and fifteen dollar bottles of wine.

"Nothing is too much trouble for you. After I collect you at the airport, we'll come back to my condo for some re-acquainting time."

Jordan pictured Darcy's arctic blue eyes that could melt her bones. "Are you suggesting we have crazy, caveman sex before we even eat?"

"Darling, please. You're making me blush."

Jordan brushed bread crumbs off the front of her hoodie. "Do I need to bring bed sheets or have you found yours?"

"The bed's all made. I'll surprise you with the colour." Darcy sounded pleased with himself.

"Probably black. Am I right?"

During the silence that followed, Jordan glanced at her watch.

Darcy cleared his throat. "I have some other news."

"Let me guess. You got my name tattooed on the cheek of your butt?"

"Now you've gone and spoiled my surprise! No, that's on my calendar for later in the week so we can get a couple's discount."

"You never cease to amaze me. Of all the activities I've imagined us doing together — that wasn't one of them."

"Actually, I hired an office assistant this morning. Her name is Kelsi Chong, and she'll run interference so you can have my undivided attention."

Jordan put the cheese back in the fridge and checked that the door was tightly closed. It had a tendency to drift open unless slammed, and she didn't want to come back to a fridge full of spoiled food. "I can't wait to meet her. Is Kelsi's office down the hall from your bedroom?"

"Certainly not. There's miles of hall and a sweeping staircase between us. And, I have a lock on my bedroom door. Not that I'll need it since I'll be sleeping with a cop."

Jordan rinsed the knife and plate and set them on the draining board. "I wasn't worried about her jumping you. But if I'm wrong, I won't be able to protect your virtue since I won't have my gun."

"Not a problem. She's almost young enough to be my daughter."

"Why didn't you say so? That would make her twelve tops, wouldn't it? I feel much better about your cozy, work arrangement now."

"Well, then. Glad that's settled. I'll see you in about three hours at the Arrivals gate. I'll be the fool tap-dancing and hooting with joy.

"I'll be sure to catch that on video." Jordan rang off and headed for the bedroom to zip her cosmetics and toiletries into her backpack.

Waiting for the taxi in front of her building, Jordan felt a thrill of excitement anticipating the erotic delights waiting for her in Darcy's arms.

Her last boyfriend, a staff sergeant from Toronto's 51 Division, turned out to be a loser. Three months into the relationship, just when she began to feel they might make it, Jordan let herself into Adam's apartment and found him in bed with a blonde Parking Enforcement officer. Adam apologized and tried to convince Jordan that it was an error of judgement he would never repeat. His pleading voice on the phone elicited a clear image of the mass of naked limbs thrashing on the bed. A year later, Jordan still didn't know whether to laugh or puke at the memory.

Here she was, on the brink of a relationship with Darcy. If she had time before boarding, she'd change her ticket to open return, just in case.

CHAPTER FIVE

Tuesday, 1:00 p.m.

DARCY RIPPED THE BED APART. BUNDLING UP THE BLACK SHEETS, he shoved them into the packing box and remade the bed with the red satin set. "She thinks she knows me," he muttered. "Can't have her think I'm predictable."

After changing clothes for the trip to the airport, he bounded down the staircase. The smell of freshly-brewed coffee drew him into the kitchen where Kelsi handed him a cup and offered him a cinnamon bun.

Darcy accepted the coffee but waved away the pastry. "*Non, merci.* Have to watch the waistline now that I've hit the big 3-0." He patted his flat abdomen.

Kelsi giggled. "Yeah, right, Mr. P." She gave an approving nod at his boot cut Armani jeans and short-sleeved Ralph Lauren shirt. "I've set up a couple of appointments for next week. On Monday, you have a 10:00 a.m. meeting with a Madame Couture."

"Ah, yes. Delightful cherub of a woman who suspects hubby is banging an associate in his law firm. Pardon my French."

"Nice," Kelsi said, as she wiped her hands on a napkin and returned to her office to retrieve the client's file.

Darcy followed and perched on the end of her desk. "When Madame Couture arrives, she'll give you a retainer of $2,000. Please give her a receipt. The book is in your locked bottom drawer."

"You got it." Kelsi spun a full circle in her chair.

Looking over Kelsi's shoulder at his appointment calendar on her computer screen, he said, "My 1:30 p.m. appointment next Tuesday is with an 80-year-old widower, Claude Deniseau. He suspects his caregiver is stealing from his bank account."

"Now, that's cold," Kelsi said with a grimace. Will he be paying me a retainer, too?"

"No, but that's the spirit. He mailed his cheque to my Montréal office last week. You'll find it in his file."

"How did you get into the private investigation business, if you don't mind me asking?"

"It was a given since my great-uncle started the firm in the 70's. I wasn't ready to jump in straight out of university. I took a year off."

Kelsi leaned forward. "What did you do? Travel around Europe? Join a protest group?"

"No. I knew I would get in plenty of travelling while apprenticing at our other offices. I did a one-year stint in Border Services at Trudeau Airport."

He shrugged at Kelsi's questioning look. "It proved interesting. I gained valuable experience learning when to trust my gut instincts and in exercising diplomacy. You better be right if you plan to accuse an incoming traveller of smuggling contraband."

"Ha! Did you conduct strip searches? Where was the most shocking place you found contraband stashed?"

"I'm not sure you're old enough for those stories. I'm going to my office to review reports from one of my operatives staking out Mr. Can't-Keep-It-In-His Pants. Could you make a dinner reservation for two, under my name, for 7:30 p.m. Friday evening at the Champlain. It's at the Château Frontenac. The number is in the computer, general file, under QC restaurants.

"Yep ... uh, I mean, *comme vous l'avez commandé, mon capitaine.*"

As Darcy's butt met the seat of his chair, his phone buzzed again.

"*Ça va?* This afternoon? I'm meeting a friend at the airport. Does it have to be today? I guess we can meet you there. Sure. *À tout a l'heure.*

Shit. This wasn't what he had in mind after picking up Jordan. However, one didn't say no to Auntie Dot. Jordan would understand.

Like hell she would.

CHAPTER SIX

Tuesday, 3:00 p.m.

LUCAS HAD ENDURED A DISTINCT *EAU DE* DOG EMANATING FROM the carpet in the visiting professors' apartment at Université Laval. He'd had enough. To celebrate the end of the Death's Reality summer course, and mark his impending retirement from academia, he checked into the luxurious Fairmont Château Frontenac. He had two full days to relax before the morgue tour. After that, home.

With a contented sigh, he settled into the padded gold and blue-striped easy chair and supported his arthritic knee on the ottoman. He couldn't put off that knee replacement much longer.

The fifth-floor suite's old world décor calmed his spirit. He shifted his chair to face the window alcove to watch the cruise ships and barges float along the majestic St. Lawrence River. The bedroom view was equally enchanting, overlooking the chef's rooftop garden. Tonight, he'd crank open the window and let the scents of lavender and mint help him sleep.

The Rococo wallpaper reminded him of the hotel he and Jolene had stayed in during their trip to France, five years ago, before they knew she was sick. He reached for the tumbler of Revel Stoke Spiced Whiskey.

He inhaled the zesty aroma and savoured the smooth taste of his drink, reflecting back to the day he presented the proposal for this grad course to the department Chair at the University of Waterloo. These days, some department heads were nervous about exposing young minds to unpleasant experiences. To Lucas's surprise, the Chair approved the proposal and welcomed the short course into the Philosophy Department's curriculum.

Choosing Université Laval to teach a summer course had given him respite from his empty home in Waterloo, where he half-expected to hear Jolene's voice calling to him from another room. Despite lecturing others on the stages of grief, he seemed irrevocably stuck in stage 2 — anger.

Enough with the self-pity. Back to work. He put on his glasses and flipped open the folder resting on his knees. Despite his lengthy teaching career, he still felt some apprehension when reading student evaluations. He breezed through fourteen forms, all providing positive comments. One student reported spotting a ghost at the cemetery they visited. Evidently, she considered that incident to be the highlight of the course. The professor shook his head and picked up the final sheet.

One word had been printed across the form in red pen. "SUCKED!!!!"

Lucas laughed out loud and reached for the whiskey bottle. Well, Mr. Jared Kavello, hope you aren't too disappointed with your failing grade.

Something white slid under the door. He hobbled over and picked up a folded sheet of paper and opened it.

Random letters had been cut from newsprint and pasted on the page. After he read the first line, he supported himself against the wall.

I'vE BeEN PaiD TO kILL YoU, PrOFEsSOR.

WHaT pRICe WoULd YoU PAY mE TO LEt yOU LIvE?

PLACe AN aD iN toMoRRow'S QUEbEC ChROnICLE UnDEr CLAsSIfIEDS. INSErT tHe FIgURe yOU'D PAy iN ThE sPAcE bELOw. If YOu cALL tHE pOLiCE, YOUr GrANdSOnS' nEW

PlAYMaTE wILL BE THe GrIM ReAPeR. THE pHONE nUmBER Is
fICtITIoUS.

    CoUNtRY lOT FOr SaLE ALOnG THe JEaN-LAROSE rIVeR
$_____. FIrm. CaLL 555-240-6767 FOr DETAiLs.

    Who would do this? Could this be from one of his students? He had
used the reference to the Grim Reaper more than once in class. Surely,
not even Kavello would stoop this low. Should he warn his son, Greg, and
leave the city tonight? Had he ever mentioned where his family lived?
There was still Friday's field trip.

    He reached for the phone to call the police. But his fingers froze. No.
Corbin's and Travis's lives could be jeopardized. He had no choice but to
follow the extortionist's instructions. His head throbbed.

    He lay on the couch with a cold, damp washcloth on his forehead in
an attempt to ease his headache. The phone clipped to his belt vibrated.
He opened an email from his friend, Dorothée Dufresne. Would he meet
her at the 1608 Wine and Cheese Bar in the Château at five o'clock? She
wanted to introduce him to someone special. Lucas hit the reply key,
ready to beg off.

    He paused. Dorothée knew he was leaving Québec City in a few days.
If he didn't meet with her and convince her that all was well, she'd hunt
him down and pry his secret from him. He accepted her invitation.

    His heart raced as he noticed the time. He used his laptop to access
the newspaper classified ads department. The English-language
Chronicle-Telegraph was a weekly newspaper, publishing Wednesdays.
Tomorrow. Twenty minutes until deadline.

    How much cash could he access by Friday? With stiff fingers, he
provided his credit card information, then typed in the phony ad details.
Three minutes to deadline, he entered a figure and hit the Submit
button.

CHAPTER SEVEN

Tuesday, 4:00 p.m.

By the look on Jordan's face, her fellow passengers were fortunate she wasn't allowed to transport her gun. Darcy had offered to pay for an upgrade to business class, but she scoffed at the expense. She didn't mind folding her long legs into steerage for the short flight from Toronto.

It was obvious that the flight didn't go smoothly. No doubt, he would hear about it in due time. Even in faded, skinny jeans and a hooded sweatshirt, with her dark hair pulled into a casual ponytail, she caused his heart rate to soar. The blood left his head and raced to places that should remain inconspicuous in public.

Jordan spotted him, and her expression softened. As they walked toward each other, Darcy sensed the crowd and its accompanying clamour disappear.

Jordan wrapped her arms around his neck and pressed her body against his. Seconds later, she pulled her head back and winked at him. "I'm happy to see you, too, cowboy. Nice hat." She reached up and tugged the black Stetson down to cover his eyes.

He repositioned the hat. "I wanted to make sure I was easy to spot." Darcy said, running his hands down her arms.

He reached for her luggage, and they headed for the exit. As he pulled away from the Jean Lesage International Airport onto rue Principale, he licked his dry lips. "We have a slight change of plan."

Her fingers had been making happy inroads on his thigh. She snatched her hand back. "You're telling me you have to work?"

He recaptured her hand and placed it on his knee, hoping it would journey north again. "I am yours, my sweet, until your flight carries you away from me on Sunday afternoon. My new assistant will ensure we are not interrupted by mundane matters."

"Then, what's the deal?"

"My favorite auntie called and summoned us to meet her and a friend for a glass of wine. An hour only, then we'll head to my place for Chinese take-out and begin our reunion celebration."

"Fine by me. I'd like to meet your aunt, and I could use a glass of wine. Listen to what happened before we took off from Toronto."

She launched into a diatribe about a man who refused to sit beside her. Of course, Jordan wouldn't move and a confrontation followed between her and the crew.

"What happened after that?"

"The crew talked some other guy into sending his wife over to sit with me, and the nut job sat with the husband. After that, the flight attendant ignored my request for tea. I plan to file a complaint with the airline."

She was probably on their no-fly list, but he wouldn't mention that now. He'd make alternate arrangements for her return flight.

They reached the old part of the city. Darcy manoeuvered through the narrow streets as they climbed the promontory towards the Château Frontenac on rue des Carrières. Jordan raised her sunglasses to get a better look at the architecture of the hotel. With its multitude of towers, turrets, and copper roof, it resembled a medieval French castle.

"Isn't she a beaut?" Darcy asked. "There's 650 rooms, and three five-star restaurants as well as the wine bar you'll see in a few moments."

Jordan whistled. "It doesn't happen often, but I'm speechless. I've only seen it in photographs."

He'd wait until they were inside the bar before giving her the scoop on his aunt.

CHAPTER EIGHT

Tuesday, 4:15 p.m.

LUCAS SPLASHED COLD WATER ON HIS FACE AND DREW IN DEEP breaths. All he could do now is wait to see if he'd paid enough to save his life.

Since he had time to kill before he was to meet Dorothée in the wine bar, a walk along the Dufferin Terrace might help relax him. The Dufferin was a river-side boardwalk, dotted with iron gazebos, separating the rear of the hotel from the steep drop to the St. Lawrence River. Stopping at the first gazebo, he gazed down the embankment at the Holland American cruise ship, "Maasdam" docked at the harbour. He would love to board and sail away to safety.

Leaning over the wrought-iron railing, Lucas glimpsed a section of the original stone rampart begun in 1608 by the French explorer, Samuel de Champlain. It was re-fortified by the victorious British invaders after a short battle on the Plains of Abraham in 1759. A hundred years later, the city returned to French rule. And we have lived an uneasy co-existence since. Two cultures never merging.

He treasured the history visible in every corner of this old part of the city. One day, he hoped to return with his grandsons to show them the framework of their heritage. The tide of sorrow that followed this thought carried him back inside the hotel, past the high-end stores selling everything from clothing to sculptures and paintings.

It was time to put on his game face.

CHAPTER NINE

Tuesday, 4:45 p.m.

"BACK UP THERE, PIERMONT. YOUR AUNT IS DOROTHÉE DUFRESNE, a Deputy Director with the Québec City Police Service?" Jordan made an effort to lower her voice. "That's like a Deputy Chief in Toronto. These white shirts all know each other from conferences and summits. Why didn't you tell me at the airport? I could have changed clothes and at least fixed my hair! Where's the bathroom?"

Darcy pointed. After she marched away, he gestured to a waiter and placed his order for the cheese selection *du jour*. He perused the wine list and chose a bottle of white wine. "The 2010 Pessac-Leognan. And a pitcher of ice water, please."

Well, they weren't off to a good start but, after she met *Tante* Dot, Jordan would realize his mother's sister was his auntie first and a Deputy Director of the SPVQ second. Or, maybe not.

He broke into a wide smile as Jordan walked toward him. Her dark hair reached her collarbone, and she had applied eye makeup and an earthy-toned lip gloss. Her well-worn sweatshirt hung over her arm. A form-fitting black camisole didn't quite meet the low-rise waistband of her jeans, allowing light from the overhead chandeliers to reflect off the silver skull stud in her belly button. Sweat beaded on his forehead, and he swiped at it with a napkin.

Jordan ignored the male heads that turned as she crossed the marble-tiled floor. She slid into the chair beside him, back to the wall. Cop-style. Jordan gulped down a glass of water and poured another.

He spotted *Tante* Dot at the bar entrance, followed by an older man with short, silver hair. Darcy stood to welcome them, reaching down to adjust the thin, red strap of Jordan's bra that had slipped over her shoulder.

She snapped, "Knock it off," before finding a smile for the newcomers. *Tante* Dot greeted them warmly. Jordan appeared uncomfortable with the double-cheek kiss she received from the other woman.

Tante Dot introduced her friend as Lucas Stride, a visiting professor from the University of Waterloo in Ontario. "Lucas's dear wife, Jolene, was my roommate at Concordia University in Montréal. We were lifelong friends until she passed away almost a year ago." She patted the professor's hand. "Lucas and I play online Scrabble once a week. He's leaving for home soon and I wanted him to meet you, Darcy." She nodded at her nephew, then smiled at Jordan, "And your lovely companion, of course. Lucas has been staying at the Château for his last week which is why I asked you both to meet us here." She re-positioned her chair to have a partial view of the room.

Darcy noticed Jordan softening a bit. "Very pleased to meet you, Professor Stride," he said. I've heard a lot about you and your wife over the years from my aunt. Was this a working visit?"

"I've been teaching a Philosophy course, *Death's Reality,* at Laval and have managed to take in some of the sights. And, please call me Lucas."

Jordan swallowed her mouthful. "Death's reality? I deal with that reality all the time. What's your take on it?"

Lucas explained the premise of the course. Jordan listened while watching the professor massage his temple.

The cheese plate held only a few crumbs of aged, white cheddar and the garnish of green grapes. Jordan made short work of both. Darcy beckoned the waiter and ordered another plate.

Lucas picked up his wineglass, then set it down without touching it to his lips. "I'm taking the class to the city morgue on Friday. Not to frighten the students, but to reinforce that we'll all end up in a body bag one day."

To fill the awkward silence following this comment, Darcy offered to order another bottle of wine.

"Not for me," his aunt advised. "I'm attending a dinner meeting at headquarters in an hour."

Darcy looked at the professor, who shook his head. "Thanks, but I have some last-minute notes to write for my final course report. As a matter of fact, I'm afraid I must leave now. It has been a pleasure to have this time with you, Dorothée, and to meet the two of you."

He shook hands with Jordan and Darcy before turning to *Tante* Dot and kissing her cheek. "We will meet tomorrow night online for our Scrabble game, dear friend."

The crinkles at the corners of his aunt's grey eyes deepened as she watched her friend leave the bar.

Darcy divided the remainder of the wine between his and Jordan's glasses. He snared a slice of local Damafro gouda, barely avoiding the cheese spreader wielded by Jordan's quick fingers.

His aunt gazed out a tall window that overlooked the blue water of the St. Lawrence River before speaking. "Darcy did you notice anything amiss with Lucas?"

Darcy pulled his eyes away from Jordan's lips as they parted to receive another cracker-load of soft cheese. "*Pardon?*"

His aunt forced a strand of dark hair back into her chignon. "About Lucas. Didn't you sense there was something serious on his mind? I hoped he would stay longer and divulge what is troubling him."

"Now that you mention it, dear aunt, I did. I only just met the man, though."

Jordan paused with the knife in her hand. "His body language suggests a high level of anxiety."

She attacked the cheese board again. When she looked up, she realized Darcy and his aunt were waiting for her to continue.

"Your concern may be justified, Madame Dufresne. You saw him rubbing at his temple. He didn't touch the food and only pretended to drink his wine. I'm not familiar with the professor's usual colouring, but his complexion appeared mottled. So, either he needs to be examined by a doctor or something serious is worrying him."

"Please call me Dorothée, Jordan. Excuse me a moment." She moved away to the window to make a call.

Darcy pulled both of Jordan's red straps up onto her shoulders. "Doesn't that bother you?"

"Not a bit." She finished off the last grape and reached for her wine. "I feel a lot better now. I was famished."

His aunt returned to their table. "Lucas assures me he has had a recent cardio exam and is in perfect health. He denies being out of sorts."

"There you go," Darcy responded. "He's fine."

"My meeting is in thirty minutes." *Tante* Dot kissed Darcy's cheeks. "I hope to see you again before you return to Toronto, Jordan. I want to hear about your work with the Guns and Gangs Task Force, especially last month's raid. The sheer number of weapons and drugs that were seized has raised the bar for every police jurisdiction in the country."

"Thanks. I'm happy to have met you, um, Dorothée." Jordan stuck her hand out for a shake before *Tante* Dot could kiss her again.

As soon as his aunt turned to leave, Darcy gestured at a waiter for the bill. He gathered Jordan's belongings and urged her to her feet. "At last, *mon petit chou*. Let's hustle our asses back to my place."

After a quick stop for takeout, they arrived at the condo. Jordan scrutinized the piano-key doorbell while Darcy opened the door and punched in the code to silence the alarm. Good, Kelsi had left for the day. He dropped the bag of food in the kitchen, bumped the suitcase up the staircase, and towed Jordan along with his free hand. "We'll eat later."

In his bedroom, she resisted his attempt to throw her on the bed. "Take it down a notch. I need a shower."

Shower? Darcy sniffed his armpit. "You use this bathroom, and I'll take the one down the hall. Meet you back here in five."

Twenty minutes later, he waited under the red satin sheet in the middle of the bed, head propped on one hand. What the hell was she doing in there?

He considered checking to see if she had fallen asleep or passed out. Who took a shower this long? She'd look like a prune.

At last. The shower head ceased its rainforest cascade. Darcy watched the door, but still no Jordan. "You okay in there?" he called.

"Fine," she responded, as she turned on her hair dryer.

Thirty-five minutes after Jordan entered the bathroom, the door opened. Darcy lounged against the pillow, adjusting the sheet over his hips.

Jordan emerged, a black bath sheet secured between her breasts. She reached back and turned off the bathroom light.

Darcy sucked in his breath. The sight and scent of her made him light-headed.

"Are you ready for this, Piermont?" With a quick tug, she let the towel fall to the floor.

Darcy groaned. "If I was any more ready, luv, I'd be downright useless. How much foreplay are you going to require?" He threw the sheet back invitingly.

"I'm good." Jordan took a running jump and landed on the bed beside him. The impact caused their bodies to slide along the slick fabric. Before Darcy could grab onto the headboard, they plummeted to the hardwood floor.

"Ow, ow. Can you move your knee?" His words came out as a gurgled plea. Her knee was rammed into his personal assets while her elbow cut off the blood supply to his carotid artery. He did feel woozy now.

"Well, shit." She released the pressure on his neck but in the process shoved her knee higher into his groin. "It's locked."

With an agonized moan, Darcy rolled out from under her. Once clear, he reached for her leg and straightened it. "There, how's that?"

"Better, thanks." She reached up, fingered the edge of the sheet, and rolled over to face him. "What's this? Don't you have anything less slippery? Like, cotton?"

"Never mind the sheets. My circulation appears to be returning. Let's stay here where it's safe."

CHAPTER TEN

Tuesday, 5:00 p.m.

SEATED ON THE TOP STEP OF THE TOURIST INFORMATION BUILDING, Jag viewed the sidewalk teeming with visitors. His eyes followed a heavy-set man in his sixties, sunburned and burdened with a number of bags from the exclusive shops in Old Québec. Jag could easily separate this old guy from a healthy portion of his net worth. There were so many ways to do it, and Jag knew them all.

Once the guy was out of sight, Jag focussed on a 30-ish woman, slim with dark hair and wearing designer sunglasses. Forget money. He pictured her naked until she disappeared around a corner.

Still a half hour until he was to meet Sherryn.

His choice to lay low in Québec City may yield better results than initially expected. The outline for Laval's *Death's Reality* course appealed to his dark side and the university rented out dorm rooms at a reasonable cost, so he had signed up. The down side was that since it was a grad course, Jag had to use his real name and provide a copy of his business degree. He wasn't worried. It wasn't like he killed anybody. The cops wouldn't bother to scan academic sites for his name. His money was already in the Caymans.

Jag descended onto the sidewalk. Pulling a twenty-dollar bill from his wallet, he dropped it into the hand of a dirty street kid, ignoring the kid's surprise. He'd been there.

Tonight, he'd order an expensive bottle of wine and leave a third of it on the table. That should impress Sherryn.

He strolled along the street, reaching the D'Orsay restaurant fashionably late. Sherryn should be frothing at the mouth by now, wondering if he was going to show up.

When he dropped into the chair opposite her, she sighed with relief. Good. Now, she'd be more anxious to please him.

———

The salmon stuck in her throat, and Sherryn had to force it down with gulps of water. Even the exquisite aroma of seasonings permeating the pub didn't give her an appetite. Jag poured more wine into her glass, checking her expression to make sure she appreciated the Trapiche Chardonnay with its sixty-dollar price tag.

He forced a forkful of lobster meat into her mouth, waiting for her to agree it was the best she'd ever had. She hated lobster, but nodded her approval.

To avoid having more of his food stuffed into her mouth, Sherryn turned her head to look outside onto rue de Buade. The cobbled street was bisected by a small park. In the centre, stood a tall iron monument of a Cardinal with flowing robes and a cherub at each corner of the base.

"So, are you in?"

Sherryn pulled her attention from the Cardinal and scrutinized Jag's sharp features. She resisted the urge to hurl herself across the table and choke the life out of him. Instead, she smiled. "Sorry? Could you repeat that?"

"For God's sake. Why weren't you listening? I don't want to repeat this a second time in here."

"Well, Jag. Sorry I zoned out. Why are you whispering?"

"Because I don't want anyone to overhear, you stupid ..." He bit off the comment and poured wine into his own glass. He held up the bottle and grunted. It was empty.

Jag captured her hand, pulling her towards him. The clashing of china against glass brought a waiter running.

The cold look in Jag's eyes sent the kid scurrying away before he could ask if they wanted dessert or coffee.

"I'm going to say this just one more time. Pay attention."

Sherryn's stomach churned at his closeness and the smell of garlic on his breath. She listened while he repeated his scheme to extort money from Professor Stride. He bragged that his plan was already in motion. He needed her to play a small part. There was no risk to her, none at all. For her minimal involvement, he would pay her five thousand dollars. He promised no one would be hurt.

This would provide her with hard evidence against him. The private investigator she hired in Montréal had tracked Jared Kavello to Québec City, and discovered he was registered for a summer course. Sherryn hurried to sign up for the same class. From the first day, she had cultivated Jag and dropped hints about her mounting debts.

"Okay, I'm in."

After dinner, Jag suggested they go back to his dorm room. She told him she felt nauseous. Not such a stretch. He left her, without offering to walk her to her car.

———

Sherryn stepped into a scalding shower to wash away the feeling of Jag's hand on her bare arm. Afterwards, she tossed her clothes into the washer to remove the cloying scent of his Drakkar Noir cologne.

Wrapped in a terry cloth robe, she avoided the right side of the couch where a demon spring lurked under the green upholstered fabric in the middle cushion. She was fortunate to have scored a furnished apartment and a roommate for her short stay in the city. She took her phone from her purse and called her mother's number in Ottawa.

"Hi Mom. How are you doing? I miss you too. Sure, I'll come over for brunch on Saturday as long as it's not served too early. I'll be leaving here around five-thirty on Friday and traffic will be heavy. I might not get to my place until eleven or later."

Sherryn picked at a thread on her housecoat while her mother chattered on about her day's activities. Stifling a yawn, she listened to her mother voice her concern — yet again — about her finances.

"Mom, please. Don't worry about next month's mortgage payment. I've established a line of credit and have been researching how to recover your savings. We may have a shot."

When she heard the front door open, she said, "I'll tell you about it when I see you. My roommate just arrived so I have to go. Love you."

"Good date?" Kelsi asked, as Sherryn put her phone down.

"Not really. What have you been up to tonight?"

"Now that I've landed a job, I've been out doing my favourite thing," Kelsi admitted, giving Sherryn an exaggerated smile and wink.

"You've been hitting on men at the Le Sacrilège pub again?"

"I wish. No. I did a little power shopping at the Centre Lebourgneuf." She waved a handful of shopping bags in front of Sherryn. "I hope I get paid before my credit card bill arrives.

"Nice. How do you like working for a private investigator?"

"Considering it's my first day, I think I'm going to like it. I can learn a lot from my new boss. He's got several international business interests, and he's not at all like you'd picture. He's cool and kind of hot.

"I'm happy for you, Kelsi. Be sure to keep me up-to-date by e-mail. I'm packed and will leave for home right after our morgue tour Friday. Hope you find a new roomie fast."

"That won't be a problem, Sher. I have a cousin who's been dying to leave Montréal and move here. So, are you going to tell me about your mystery date?" Kelsi rested her bags on the arm of a decrepit easy chair.

"No, because he's not worth the energy to describe him or our date." Sherryn worked at keeping the disgust from her tone.

"He's married, right? Don't tell me you're dating Professor Stride."

"You got me. Didn't realize you knew about my daddy fixation," Sherryn said, throwing Kelsi a mischievous grin.

"Don't lie to me." Kelsi picked up her shopping treasures and started down the hall.

Sherryn called out a warning. "Don't fall over the boxes ..."

"Ouch. Too late!" Kelsi yelled.

Sherryn reached for the T.V. remote to watch the doom and gloom of the eleven o'clock news. Anything to take her mind off Jag and his scheme. Despite his assurances, a lot could go wrong.

CHAPTER ELEVEN

Wednesday, 4:00 p.m.

AFTER A DAY OF WANDERING THE STREETS, PRETENDING AN interest in history, Lucas was exhausted. He headed back to the Frontenac and pushed open the door to his suite. Another folded page waited for him on the carpet.

The weekly Chronicle-Telegraph came out that afternoon. Lucas picked up the note and inhaled deeply before unfolding it.

I aCcEPT YoUR OfFER. aN EmPTY BOdY bAG WiLL bE IN tHE MOrGuE HALLwaY. StUFF ThE $30,000 cASh In It AfTEr ThE tOUR oN FrIDaY – tHEn LEAvE!

A wave of relief washed over him. Knee throbbing, he limped to the living room desk and opened up his laptop. Time to access his bank accounts and transfer the funds. He would pick up the cash tomorrow morning at a local branch.

The iron grip of fear slowly ebbed from his body. Feeling more courageous, he vowed to report this crime when he returned home, once he ensured his grandsons' safety. The police wouldn't get his money back, but at least he could prompt an investigation.

He poured a glass of his spiced whiskey and slumped into the armchair. He closed his eyes and allowed his subconscious mind to drift. The daylight outside the window darkened to evening.

The question remained. How could he ensure his safety and that of his family? He doubted the thief followed a code of ethics.

He called his son in Toronto and gave him a sanitized version of the situation. Lucas would put enough money in Greg's account to take his wife and sons on a two-week vacation to a northern resort. Yes, he told Greg, the police were involved, and they hoped for a speedy end to the matter.

He emptied the last of the whiskey into his glass. Kicking off his shoes, he lay back on the bed. There was no turning back. The next two days of waiting would be unbearable.

Forgetting his online Scrabble date with Dorothée, he fell into an uneasy asleep. His snores drowned out the sound of his phone ringing in the sitting room.

It was morning before he noticed the red message light blinking from the hotel phone beside his bed.

CHAPTER TWELVE

Friday, 6:30 a.m.

JORDAN WOKE UP ALONE IN DARCY'S BED BETWEEN WHITE COTTON sheets that provided more traction than the red satin set. What had the man been thinking that first night? She looked at the clock on the bedside table and moaned. What the hell? She rolled over to face the bathroom door. No sound of running water or off-key singing.

Tired after two days of sightseeing, rich food, and hours in Darcy's arms, Jordan went back to sleep.

She opened her eyes at a more civilized hour and headed for the bathroom. Downstairs, the sound of drawers opening and closing drew her to the reception area. She came to an abrupt halt at the entrance.

Kelsi, she assumed, with her head down, sorted through a stack of papers on the desk. The young woman looked up, her arm jerking involuntarily, causing a stack of files to spew their contents onto the floor.

"Shit! I mean darn." She crouched and scooped up a handful of paper. "Good morning. I'm Kelsi. What can I do for you?"

"Not a thing, I'm just looking for Darcy. I'm Jordan Blair." She squatted to help with the cleanup.

"Right, Mr. P. told me you'd be visiting. Funny, we haven't run into each other before now. But, I guess you two left the condo the last couple of mornings before I got here."

With her usual bluntness, Jordan asked, "Why are you working at this hour of the morning?"

"I have to leave early this afternoon for the final lecture in my summer course. I'm making up the time, even though Mr. P. said it wasn't necessary."

Kelsi, still scrabbling for papers on the floor, looked up when Darcy rounded the corner and turned to pick up a sheet of paper. Her eyes travelled upward and stalled on the Union Jack tattoo on his left calf. Then roved to the other leg where the horns of a pawing bull met the hem of his shorts.

Jordan coughed to hide her amusement. When she met Darcy a few months ago in Honduras, she hadn't been impressed. Tattooed body, expensive clothes, and extensive international travel experience. In her line of work, that combination often spelled trouble.

"I thought I heard voices." Darcy reached his hand over to help Jordan to her feet. Slipping his arm around her waist, he said, "Kelsi, you're making me look like a slave driver."

"Sorry. Didn't want to get behind with work. I'll be leaving around three-thirty to make my last class."

"I appreciate your work ethic, but I don't want to see you here when we return from sight- seeing."

"You won't. I promise."

Darcy pulled Jordan into the kitchen. While he poured her a cup of coffee, she asked, "How is your Mom doing these days?"

"As well as can be expected, I guess. It's been a year since Dad's parachuting accident, yet at times, I still feel his presence."

Jordan pressed her cheek against his chest and hugged him. "It's hard to accept losing a parent who was only in his fifties."

"That it was. We couldn't stand the thought of putting him in the ground."

Jordan pulled back. "So you ...put him someplace else?"

Darcy pointed to the round stained-glass window set into the ceiling over the dining area. As the sun beamed through the sky light, the walls and floor reflected shades of deep blue, green, red. and amber.

"What!"

"I had a portion of his ashes mixed into the glass in this window. I think he's mostly in the blue and red," Darcy explained, and danced his fingers along the quartz counter to capture the jewel-like colours.

A mouthful of coffee burned Jordan's throat as she gulped it down. "What a bizarre ... I mean bizarrely brilliant idea. I've heard of incorporating a loved one's ashes into a sun dial, but this is the first time I've seen anything like this."

"I toyed with hiring an artist to sterilize his cremains and mix them with tattoo ink, but settled on this option instead."

Topic change coming up. "Okay, then. Where are we going for breakfast?"

"This morning, I'm taking you to Le Couchon Dingue. You'll adore their crêpes. Then, we'll do whatever you want, since you have already hiked the ramparts, inspected the changing of the guard, and viewed countless churches."

"Doesn't *couchon dingue* mean crazy pig? I expect I can get some bacon with my crêpes?"

Darcy caressed her hips. "*Oui.* You have no idea how a woman with a voracious appetite turns me on."

Jordan shoved him away. "Is that supposed to be a compliment?"

"But of course. You're a hard woman. Lucky for you I'm your slave. Now, we have several options for the rest of the day. We can hop on the "Louis Jolliet" cruise ship that sails up the St. Lawrence River past Montmorency Falls and Orleans Island. We can take in the beautiful scenery, sip wine, and gaze into each other's eyes."

"Kind of hard to look at the scenery and into each other's eyes at the same time," Jordan remarked, standing on tip-toes to nip his ear.

"Or, we can take a double-decker bus tour. Then, there's the ever-popular carriage ride. We can do any or all of these." He pressed her against the counter and covered her mouth with his.

When they paused for air, Jordan suggested, "While I'm considering these choices, let's check upstairs. I may have forgotten to make up your bed."

"Thank God for that."

CHAPTER THIRTEEN

Friday, 4:00 p.m.

LUCAS ADJUSTED THE STRAP OF HIS COMPUTER BAG TO EASE THE
weight of the cash. His pulse raced like he'd run a marathon by the time
he reached his car. He needed this nightmare to end.

In the morgue parking lot, he sat for several minutes to compose
himself. When he joined his students milling around the back door, he
forced a smile and ushered them inside. He hoped no one offered to help
him with his cumbersome bag. He searched the faces of the group.
Which one of his students was doing this to him?

A sign stating, *"Personnel autorisé seulement"* was mounted on an inside
door. Lucas pressed a buzzer set into the wall.

A woman in her forties, wearing a white lab coat, greeted the group
and escorted them inside. The temperature dropped by at least ten
degrees. All chatter ceased.

The coroner, Dr. Aurore Colet, stood beside a spotless aluminum
table with raised edges. Steel faucets attached to plastic drain hoses
gleamed under the overhead fluorescent light. Dr. Colet nodded at Lucas
and waited while the students gathered into a loose semi-circle, well

back from the table. A surgical mask dangled below the collar of her sky-blue scrubs. Her grey-streaked brown hair was pulled back into a bun, and her light blue eyes moved from face to face, as if noting the emotions written there.

"Greetings, Professor Stride and welcome students." Her tone was light and her English impeccable, with a slight French accent. She smiled reassuringly at the students and motioned them closer.

Acknowledging the woman who had shown them in, Dr. Colet said, "This is my assistant, Maria. I'm pleased to have you visit my morgue. I'll begin by explaining the procedures taken prior to and during an autopsy. There will be time for questions when I'm done." Dr. Colet paused to glance at her audience.

"As you are aware, an autopsy is conducted to determine the cause of death for legal, educational, or research purposes. The autopsy rate has dropped from 50 percent to less than 10 percent over the past fifty years. People who die in a hospital and have a doctor's signature on the Death Certificate don't come to me unless there's evidence of foul play. An autopsy can be restricted to a specific organ or include the brain and all other organs. The body is opened in a manner that doesn't interfere with an open casket service if there is to be one."

Lucas noticed several students staring at the tray of autopsy tools on Dr. Colet's side of the table. He counted heads. Fourteen. That insolent braggart, Jared Kavello, blew off the final class. Kavello wasn't getting a passing grade anyway, especially after his deportment and attitude. If Lucas had to guess the identity of his tormentor, that young bastard would top the list. But, if that was the case, why wasn't he here to collect the money?

Dr. Colet noticed the professor's frown and lack of focus. "Is there anything you wish to add, Professor Stride?"

Lucas flushed with embarrassment and caught himself from stumbling over the computer bag resting beside his foot. "Not at all, Doctor. Please continue."

"A new bag or sheet is used for each body. Plastic bags are placed over the hands of the deceased at the scene. Body bags are closed and sealed to prevent any contamination or loss of evidence during transport. If the death is suspicious or undetermined, or for accidents such as drownings, or if the individual was in custody prior to death, they end up on my table. If the autopsy is not performed immediately, the body will be refrigerated. Maria will give you a tour of that area when I'm finished." A thin smile crossed her lips at the lack of enthusiasm exhibited by the students.

Even though the autopsy room was cold enough to raise goose bumps on bare flesh, Lucas retrieved a handkerchief to wipe perspiration from his face and neck. He struggled to listen to Dr. Colet's words.

"The bag is opened and the body is photographed *in situ*. In a forensic autopsy, I note the clothing of the deceased and the position of the clothing. Samples of foreign objects, any residues or fibers, hair, and fingernail scrapings are collected here."

As the lecture continued, Lucas noticed Sherryn reach out and clutch Kelsi's hand. The graphic wording, in addition to the pungent odour of formaldehyde and bleach, appeared to be affecting her. Lucas watched the colour drain from Sherryn's face. He was about to offer assistance when Kelsi put an arm around her shoulders. Sherryn straightened up and offered Kelsi a weak smile.

"In some cases, we use a special UV radiation to detect secretions on the skin or clothes. After the evidence is collected, the body is removed from the bag and undressed. Any wounds are examined prior to the body being cleaned, weighed, and measured. At this point, features are noted such as race, sex, hair colour and length, eye colour, approximate age and any identifying features like scars, tattoos, birthmarks, or bruises."

Dr. Colet pointed to a block on the table. "A rubber or plastic body block or brick is placed under the corpse's shoulders so the chest protrudes forward."

She picked up a scalpel from the instrument tray with a gloved hand. "At this point, I make a 'Y' incision from the shoulders to the pubic bone." She leaned forward, making three slashing motions above the imaginary corpse. One of the students gagged and turned away.

"I peel back the skin and muscle and remove the organs. They are weighed and examined macroscopically, then sliced for investigation microscopically to determine injury or disease respectively. On average, a full autopsy takes me about 50 minutes."

The doctor replaced the scalpel on the tray and surveyed the group. "Any questions?"

She acknowledged Sherryn's raised hand. "Dr. Colet, I'm feeling a little dizzy. May I be excused?"

"Of course. There is a stool in the corridor if you would like to sit down."

Lucas put his hand on Sherryn's shoulder as she passed him and spoke in a hushed tone. "I hope you feel better. You've done very well."

Sherryn's effort to smile failed. She clamped her lips together and bolted for the door.

After the question period, Maria led the students to the next room where refrigerated drawers contained the remains of the dead. Lucas stayed behind with Dr. Colet.

He listened politely to the coroner's animated account of the two weeks' she had booked off to join Doctors Without Borders, working in Syria. He was relieved when his students emerged from the cadaver storage area, rubbing their arms to restore body temperature. This was the last time he would see them, and the end of their introduction to the realities of death. Did they have a better appreciation for life and the necessity of making the most of every day they were granted? Time would tell.

CHAPTER FOURTEEN

Friday, 5:30 p.m.

LUCAS THANKED DR. COLET AND MARIA FOR THEIR TIME AND ushered his subdued group from the building. After closing the metal door, he looked around the corridor. Satisfied he was alone, he shot the bolt in case a straggler returned to ask a question of the medical examiner. Highly unlikely but best to be sure.

Along one wall, a shelving unit held bundles of thick, black vinyl. Body bags. His gaze slid to the nearby stretcher. A long bag lay on top, the zipper open suggestively. With a glance around the anteroom, Lucas moved closer to the stretcher.

Was that a footstep? Lucas listened but heard only the rhythmic ticking of an old clock mounted on the wall. His heartbeats thudded in his throat. He swallowed with difficulty and dropped his computer bag on the stretcher. He pulled out a bundle of cash to shove into the body bag. When he reached for the second bundle, his hand froze in mid-air. He was sure he heard something. A rustling.

A door creaked open behind him. Lucas dropped the packet of money onto the stretcher and spun around to confront a figure, standing motionless in the corridor. The face was concealed by a balaclava. Dressed in dark pants and oversized sweatshirt, the slight figure could be male or female.

Seconds passed. Either this masked person had stayed behind when the others left, or he — or she — had been in the building all along, waiting to take the money. Sherryn had left the class early. She hadn't visited the cadaver storage room. Could it be ...? No, not Sherryn.

The figure advanced. The gait was that of a man.

Lucas found his voice. "Here's the money, you low-life son-of-a-bitch. Threatening my grandchildren and my life so you can live off money I earned. Don't think you'll get away with this!"

The silent figure moved closer. Lucas reached up and grabbed a fistful of the mask and yanked it up.

He was right. Lucas stumbled backwards at the sight of Kavello's malevolent expression.

"I've notified the police. They're on their way. Did you really think you could pull this off?."

Kavello scoffed. "Your word against mine, Dr. Death. My boring classmates will confirm I didn't attend the lecture."

Lucas waved the balaclava at Kavello. "I have this." He stuffed it into his pocket. "Plenty of DNA here. If you're as smart as you think you are, you'll leave my money and make a run for it."

Kavello grabbed Lucas, shoving him against the gurney. Lucas struggled but couldn't break free. Kavello's youth made it an uneven match.

A forearm circled Lucas's throat, cutting off his attempts to call for help. He couldn't inhale. As the arm tightened, the pressure in his head increased and darkness crept across his peripheral vision. His body was wrenched aside and hauled backwards down the hall.

Terror gripped him. Rational thought vanished. He flailed his right arm in an attempt to gouge Kavello's face. With his left hand, he tried to relieve the pressure from around his neck. He was dragged through a door, then into the fluorescent light of the men's room.

Confronting Kavello had been a deadly mistake. The door closed behind them.

His vision narrowed to a pinprick, then extinguished.

He heard Kavello's fading voice in his ear. "Hope you left behind a fucking awesome footprint, Professor."

CHAPTER FIFTEEN

Friday, 5:40 p.m.

THIS WAS NO TIME TO LOSE HER NERVE. SHERRYN SPLASHED HER FACE with cold water and groped for a paper towel.

Jag had warned her that timing was critical to pulling this off. If one of the morgue staff found the money before she got to it, everything she had had to do — from cultivating Jag's repugnant company to hiring a detective and moving to Québec City — was for nothing. The question of why he needed her in the first place was not difficult to decipher. She was his scapegoat in case the professor informed the police. Too late to back out now.

Sherryn placed her ear against the door. Silence. She opened it and stuck her head into the hall. Clear. She had to move fast.

She raced to the gurney. Stacks of cash spilled from an open computer bag. The professor's transfer of money had been interrupted.

Fingers shaking, Sherryn shovelled the cash into her backpack and threw it over her shoulder. Checking she was still alone, she stuffed the professor's bag into a waste receptacle beside the stretcher.

She hit the bar on the exit door. Her head slammed against the metal. Damn, it was bolted. After fumbling with the release, she shoved it open and ran across the parking lot, unlocking her SUV.

Tossing her backpack onto the passenger seat, she scrambled inside and threw the Forester into reverse. A fist pounded on the back window. She slammed the gear shift into drive and glanced back. Jag stood beside her vehicle, his face contorted with rage. She floored the gas pedal, cornering left onto the street, swerving around a semi that was pulling out from the transport company behind the morgue. The driver laid on his horn, and the noise ripped at her frayed nerves as she drove along rue Décory. With luck, the transport would slow Jag down.

A red traffic light forced her to hit the brakes.

She stared into her rear-view mirror, happy to see a second transport truck pulling onto the road, blocking the parking lot exit. A horn blasted from the vehicle behind her.

She hit Go on her GPS, having pre-set the address of police headquarters.

———

Jag ran for his car in the back row of the morgue parking lot. He shot onto the street, slamming his brakes to avoid the transport truck blocking the intersection.

He thumped the steering wheel with his palms, then leaned on the horn. He shoved his hand out the window, and gave the driver a one-fingered salute.

When the road cleared, Jag followed in the transport's wake. Sherryn had a five-minute start on him. His head was going to explode. The urge to ram the truck in front of him was overwhelming. Instead, he took the first exit ramp.

He waited a half hour in front of Laval's library building where they had agreed to meet. Sherryn told him she was going to drive straight on to Ottawa after he handed over her $5,000 — as though that was ever part of his plan. Now she had all the money. He'd find her and make her regret double-crossing him.

CHAPTER SIXTEEN

Friday, 6:00 p.m.

SHERRYN'S STRATEGY HAD BEEN TO FIND INCRIMINATING documents that she could present to the Ottawa Police Fraud Section. It had been a long shot from the start. But, she was driven by the need to see Jag arrested for defrauding her parents of their entire investment portfolio. Her dad struggled with depression all his life, and watching their nest egg disintegrate without legal recourse had been too much for his fragile emotional state. His solution was suicide. Sherryn was glad he would never know what she did to ensure payback for Jag.

When Jag wheedled her into picking up the ransom from Professor Stride, she saw this as her opportunity to prove he was a crook.

He shouldn't have been inside the morgue. Guess they both changed the agenda. Too bad she hadn't backed over the bastard when she had the chance.

She parked in the lot at the Poste de Police. Before climbing out, she checked again to ensure Jag hadn't caught up to her. There was no sign of him. With the backpack cradled in her arms, she ran up the steps.

After reporting the crime of extortion to the desk officer with her limited French, she was advised to sit on a bench and wait. When Constable Bonnet returned, he escorted her into an interview room where an attractive woman in civvies sat in a chair behind a battered wooden table. The constable stood at ease by the door.

The woman scarcely glanced at Sherryn. "Good afternoon, Miss Groves. I am Detective-Sergeant Nicoline Perrot. Please provide more details about this alleged crime."

Sherryn dropped the backpack, opened it, and turned it upside down. Bundles of cash cascaded across the table.

———

After leaving the police station, Sherryn figured the chances of getting money back for her mother were slim. At least, she could make Jag's life miserable in the attempt. Next hurdle would be to find enough money for a lawyer to fight the defense Jag was sure to mount.

Before starting her Forester, she called home. "Hi, Mom. I'm behind schedule. I need to make a quick stop at the apartment before heading out."

Her mother wished her a safe drive.

Sherryn said, "I'll explain what held me up tomorrow. See you then."

She cranked up the volume on an easy rock FM station. She would have preferred not to return to her apartment at all, but she needed to warn Kelsi in case Jag showed up there. She should have asked for a police officer to accompany her.

She called Kelsi. No answer. She left a message for her friend to get out of the apartment immediately and wait for her in the bistro across the street from the building. She'd try again from the lobby to make sure Jag wasn't inside. Then, she and Kelsi would get the hell away until the dickhead was apprehended.

CHAPTER SEVENTEEN

Friday, 7:00 p.m.

WAS THE PROFESSOR DEAD? MENTALLY, JAG RETRACED HIS STEPS, FROM plan formulation to execution — he snickered to himself at his word choice. Then, he sobered again. Sherryn was the only link to the professor that could incriminate him.

Pulling away from the library, and into the evening traffic, he drove towards Sherryn's apartment building, glad he had followed her home once. He would check for her car. Unlikely she'd return to her apartment, but it was worth a try.

Her SUV wasn't in her parking spot. Should he wait, or cut his losses and get out of town? He visualised the bitch enjoying the money he worked for.

She may have been here and gone, or not come back at all. Or, maybe she was driving around afraid he was on her tail.

An overflowing dumpster in the back corner of the lot provided cover for the Taurus. When he rolled down his window, the smell of rotting garbage from the dumpster churned his stomach, but he left it open. He needed to listen for an incoming vehicle.

Intermittent traffic from the street covered the approach of a tenant carrying a bulging bag of garbage. Jag tensed, but the man tossed the bag and returned to the building.

Jag frowned at his watch. She wasn't coming. He was tempted to break into Sherryn's apartment but recalled she had a roommate. He could check, though, and whether the roommate was home or not, force his way in to look for his money.

A set of headlights turned into the lot from the street. He got out of his car and eased the door closed.

The SUV parked in Sherryn's spot and the headlights died. She got out, phone to her ear. As soon as she turned to lock the vehicle, he jumped her.

With one arm, he grabbed her around the neck from behind and squeezed off her gurgled scream. He buried his free hand in her hair and dragged her backwards. The keys fell from her fingers, and her phone dropped to the gravel.

He released his hold on her hair, placed his hand over her mouth, and shoved her up against her vehicle. She bit his hand. He jerked it away and slapped her across the face.

Pressing his lips to her ear, he whispered, "What? Not glad to see me?

"What do you think? Asshole!" She wiped blood from the corner of her mouth.

"Trying to run off with all the cash? Bitch! Where's my money?"

When she responded with a whimper, he punched her in the abdomen. She doubled over and fell to the ground, then got to her hands and knees and crawled towards the building. He grabbed her ankle and dragged her back to him.

"I'm not going to ask you again."

He drew her upright and squeezed her jaw, forcing her to look into his eyes.

"Answer me!" He felt a surge of pleasure as tears and blood streamed down Sherryn's face. He released her jaw so she could answer.

"I d-don't have it."

"Where is it?"

Jag looked over his shoulder to ensure they were still alone. Sherryn scrapped her shoe down his shin bone. He yelped, but maintained his hold on her. Grimacing through clenched teeth, he warned, "Give me the money, or you'll regret it."

"Don't have it."

Jag smashed his fist into her temple. She dropped to the ground. He aimed a volley of kicks to her ribs, forcing himself to stop when lights came on in a second floor window.

He picked up her keys and opened the rear hatch. After searching through the suitcases and boxes, he spotted a backpack on the passenger seat. He dove across the console to nab it.

Jag pawed through the contents, finding only the crap women drag around with them. He hunted under the front and back seats. Nothing.

Climbing out, he prodded Sherryn's limp body with his foot. No response. He hauled her into the back seat, cramming her body between a pile of text books and a laptop. Jag would have thrown her into the dumpster, but the sides were too high. He locked the doors before tossing her keys.

He flexed his skinned fist and gave her rear tire a parting kick.

He needed to calm down and get out of the city. The professor's thirty grand was peanuts compared to his holdings in offshore accounts. As the adrenaline ebbed, it occurred to him that he should check one more place.

CHAPTER EIGHTEEN

Friday, 6:30 p.m.

DARCY ZIPPED JORDAN'S DRESS AND LEANED DOWN TO KISS THE NAPE of her neck. "I'm going to miss you."

"I'm not gone yet. We still have two nights and two days." Jordan smoothed the black dress over her hips, and asked, "Will I do for this fancy place you're taking me to?"

"No one will look at the other women there. I fear a middle-eastern prince or a British earl will lure you away from me."

Jordan knuckled him in the chest. "I'm into tattooed P.I.s these days. You're safe for now."

"Smashing." Darcy rubbed his chest "Just let me get my jacket and we'll be off. There should be time for a drink before dinner."

His ring tone sounded from his pocket. "It's *Tante* Dot. Sorry, I better get this."

Without a greeting, his aunt said, "I hope I haven't called at an inconvenient time. I need a favour."

Darcy glanced at Jordan standing before the dresser mirror clutching a handful of errant hair as though wondering what to do with it. "Of course. My favorite aunt has only to ask, and it is done. Do you need me to dispose of a body?"

"You're a strange boy, Darcy, but I love you anyway. Lucas didn't meet me online Wednesday night for our Scrabble game. I've left numerous messages, but he hasn't returned my calls. He conducted his last class this afternoon at the morgue and planned to stay one more night at the Château before heading home tomorrow morning."

"He's probably having a last night out on the town. I'm sure he's fine. I can tell you're worried, though, so what can I do to help?" Darcy groaned inwardly as he made the offer. Dinner reservations were for seven-thirty, an hour from now.

"There's more I need to tell you. I just called Lucas's son in Toronto. Greg received a disconcerting message from his father on Wednesday evening. Lucas said someone threatened him and his family. Greg told me his father had informed the police of the threat, but we have had no such report here. I contacted the Waterloo Regional Police, and they know nothing of it either."

Darcy tried to interrupt to ask a question, but reconsidered due to the urgency of his aunt's tone.

"I called the morgue to confirm Lucas's lecture was conducted as planned. The night attendant consulted the activity log. Lucas and his students were signed out at 5:30 p.m."

"I can see why you're upset." Darcy eyed Jordan's sleek silhouette in the clinging dress and forced his attention back to his aunt.

"An official search cannot yet be initiated for Lucas. And, I have another damnable meeting this evening that may well go past midnight. Could you stop by the Château and try to locate him?"

"Of course. Glad to. As it happens, Jordan and I have dinner reservations at the Champlain restaurant. We'll take a stroll around the hotel and, when we find the good professor, ask him to call you."

"Thank you, Darcy. His suite number is 5147. Please report back to me whether you locate Lucas or not. I'll keep my cell on vibrate during the meeting. And, give my fondest regards to Jordan. I regret intruding on your evening."

"Not to worry, *Tante* Dot." Darcy disconnected and turned to Jordan.

"Sorry, darling, my aunt has asked me to run old Lucas to ground. We'll scout around for him before dinner."

Jordan picked up her silver evening bag. "I got the gist of the conversation. If he's not in his room, we'll check the boardwalk. Can you push our reservation back a half hour?"

———

At the Château Frontenac's front entrance, Darcy watched the doorman pretend to avert his eyes from Jordan's legs as she slid from the seat of his Acura. The tight dress made it impossible for her to step down without flashing her white panties.

They took the elevator to the professor's floor and followed the sign to a set of seven steps. At the top, a short, private hallway ended at a door marked with a brass plaque.

"Suite 5147. Here we are." Darcy rapped softly. After a moment, he hammered the door with his fist. He placed his ear close to the jamb and listened intently. "No sound. Keep watch for me, will you, luv?"

Before Jordan could protest, Darcy pulled a miniature metal box from his pocket and chose a tool. "Anybody coming?"

Jordan returned to the bottom of the steps and peered around the corner. "No. Elevator area is clear. What are you doing with a lock release kit? Never mind, don't answer that. I hope you realize I could lose my job if we're caught."

"The 'we' in that sentence gives me chills of pleasure, my queen. No worries. I'm a professional."

He loved her sarcastic snorts, even if most were aimed at him.

"Is lock-picking taught at snoop school?" Jordan gave the hem of her dress a yank and craned her neck towards the bank of elevators.

"Nope. I'm self-taught in this particular skill." He heard the lock disengage. "Here we go."

Stepping back to allow her to enter ahead of him, he called out, "Professor, it's Darcy and Jordan come to visit."

Still no response.

Papers lay spread across the coffee table. A laptop sat on a French

Provincial writing desk. Beside the armchair, a crystal glass shared an end table with an empty whiskey bottle. Clearly, Professor Stride hadn't checked out early.

From another pocket, Darcy pulled out two pairs of black nitrile gloves, handing one pair to Jordan.

She moved into the bedroom, leaving Darcy to pick through the scattered papers in the sitting room.

Jordan called out to him. "Two pieces of luggage are stacked in the closet and his clothing is in the drawers."

Next, he heard her voice from the bathroom. "Shaving items beside the sink. Is this a frigging bidet?"

"Look here," he said to her when she appeared at his side. "Most of this stuff is course material, but there's this." He handed her two sheets of paper, newsprint letters pasted on them.

Jordan took the pages between her gloved fingers and read them. "It's an extortion demand and a murder threat. Holy shit! Your aunt's friend is in more trouble than we thought. I guess it's too much to hope that the dirtbag left his or her prints on it."

"I'm going to call ..." Darcy reached for his cell. It rang before he could press a number.

"Auntie. What's happened?" Jordan pressed her face against his to eavesdrop.

"Darcy. I've just had a report from the afternoon shift. A man's body was discovered in the men's washroom at the city morgue at 6:05 p.m. Theft wasn't a factor. Preliminary examination suggests asphyxiation."

She choked on her next words, so Darcy helped her out. "It's Professor Stride, isn't it, Auntie?"

"Yes. Lucas is dead."

CHAPTER NINETEEN

Friday, 7:45 p.m.

"THAT POOR MAN." JORDAN DROPPED THE NOTES ON THE TABLE. "Let's go. I'm surprised the police aren't here yet."

She picked up her evening bag and ran for the door, calling over her shoulder. "Your fingerprints are on the doorknobs. Wipe both sides and move it."

Jordan waited while Darcy used the hem of his shirt to remove his prints. When he was finished, he closed the door gently, and they descended the steps to the main hallway. Jordan turned the corner towards the elevators, pulling off the nitrile gloves, stuffing them and Darcy's pair in her bag.

She heard the ping of the elevator coming to a stop on their floor and shoved Darcy in the opposite direction. "Over there into the stairwell."

The door closed behind them a split second after they heard the muted thump of feet on thick carpet, climbing the stairs to the professor's suite. When they reached the lobby level, Darcy said, "I can't believe you moved that fast in three-inch heels."

Jordan shot him a murderous look, but didn't reply. She straightened her dress and ran a hand through her hair before entering the lobby.

Once seated at a window table in the Champlain restaurant, appetizers and entrées ordered, and glasses of white wine placed before them, Jordan slipped her shoes off and flexed her toes. "If I hang around with you long enough, my career will meet a spectacularly nasty end."

With her heart rate slowing, her fury at Darcy fizzled into annoyance at herself for entering the suite.

"How can you say that, my darling? You have to admit we have exciting adventures. I hope you like this wine. It's a Cuvée Bacchus from France. Later, we can try a local sparkling Bulle de Neige."

Ass. "Whatever. Just to remind you, I can't distinguish between wines." Jordan upended her crystal wineglass and drained it. She pressed her abused, bare feet against the cool tiles.

Darcy's eyes flashed with amusement. "I could say that, if you enjoyed the better wines only, you would be unable to go back to the plonk. But, I won't, since you seem to be in pissed-off mode."

Jordan plucked the bottle from the ice and poured herself another glass. The hovering waiter rushed over to help her, but it took only one of her minor stink-eyes to send him back into the shadows.

"Do you understand what would have happened if we had been a minute later getting out of that suite?"

"I admit it would have been mildly embarrassing to have Auntie's favourite nephew found in the hotel room of a murder victim. Especially, without a pass key. Since we have alibis, our presence there would have delayed our dinner, nothing more."

The cheeky snoop refused to be contrite. "How do you know we have alibis for the time the professor died?"

Darcy waited until their server deposited the appetizers on the table — Magdalen Islands scallops for him, Old Rum Terrine of foie gras for Jordan — before answering.

"Even in a morgue, a corpse cannot lounge about on the men's room floor for long without questions being raised. The student tour ended at 5:30 p.m. The body was discovered shortly after six o'clock. Therefore, the professor died between 5:30 and 6:00 p.m. Autopsy will confirm that.

We were buying you a pair of Alexander McQueen boots at that time. The receipt should still be in your purse since you wouldn't let me buy them for you."

"You better be right. I can't be dragged into an out-of-province investigation."

She reached across and snagged a scallop from Darcy's plate. Where was her damned grilled prime beef?

She finished off the wine as their entrées were delivered. The bottle was replaced by another. Darcy's promised sparkling wine grown from grapes in *la belle province*, she assumed.

While she cleaned up the last bites of her meat and Yukon gold potatoes, Darcy answered his phone.

His eyes widened after checking the number on the screen. "Kelsi?"

The truffle sauce was to die for. Jordan used a teaspoon to scoop the last of it into her mouth as she listened.

"Kelsi?" He looked at the display a second time.

"Is something wrong with Kelsi?" Jordan asked. She suspected she wasn't getting dessert tonight. She shoved her feet back into the killer shoes.

"Don't know. Line's open but she doesn't respond. I'll get her address from my contacts' list." He poked at his phone, then motioned to the server before wolfing a last bite of his Icelandic Cod. "Let's go. Something's wrong."

Darcy threw cash on the table and hurried to the lobby, urging Jordan along. He paced as they waited for his vehicle to be brought to the front door.

"What's going on," Jordan demanded. "Could she have ass-dialled you?"

"Not sure. We'll start by checking her apartment." Darcy fiddled with the GPS on his dash.

After that bountiful dinner, Jordan longed to go back to Darcy's condo and put on her sweats. And, throw her shoes in the trash.

Darcy's little assistant better not be fabricating a damsel in distress scenario. "She knows I'm still in town, right?"

CHAPTER TWENTY

Friday, 9:30 p.m.

THE DOOR OF HIS ASSISTANT'S GROUND FLOOR APARTMENT STOOD AJAR several inches. Darcy pushed on it and called out softly, "Kelsi, are you home? It's Darcy and Jordan. Are you alright?" They heard a thump and, from a different direction, quiet moans.

Jordan grabbed Darcy's wrist and pointed to the kitchen. They discovered Kelsi bound to a chair with duct tape, a piece covering her mouth. Eyes wide with fright, she motioned with her head in the direction of the bedrooms. She squirmed on the chair as if she was sitting on a hot, metal roof. Or she badly needed the washroom.

Darcy raised his index finger to his lips and gently worked the tape from her mouth.

Kelsi squeezed her eyes shut during the process. She winced and touched the irritated skin.

Jordan used a knife from the counter to slice through the tape at Kelsi's wrists and ankles. She whispered, "Are you alone?"

Kelsi shook her head and pointed toward the bedrooms. "Jag Kavello. He's tossing our apartment."

"Stay here," Jordan ordered and tightened her grip on the knife. A baton and her Glock would be useful right now.

With Darcy close behind, she kicked off her shoes and led the way, staying close to the wall. She motioned at Darcy to check the first bedroom while she continued to the end of the hall and opened a door.

The compact bathroom appeared empty. As she pivoted to join Darcy, the shower curtains billowed outward. A figure struck Jordan on the temple with a bathroom plunger. The rubber end bounced off her head and knocked her to the floor between the tub and the toilet. The knife flew out of her hand and slid along the tiles.

The assailant dropped the plunger and leaped for the open window above the tub. Jordan backed out of the tight space and jumped up. She dove forward, and grabbed for his feet, catching him by one ankle. He kicked at her with his free leg, catching her shoulder, spinning her around. He disappeared over the window ledge.

Now she was pissed. Darcy burst into the room as she pulled herself through the window sill. She yelled over her shoulder, "Go out the front and around the side of the building."

Jordan dropped to the sidewalk that rimmed the parking lot. She saw Kavello weaving through rows of cars in the direction of a dumpster. She chased him barefoot, ignoring the rough gravel as she pounded after him. He dashed around the dumpster and opened his car door. She grasped the handle as the lock engaged. The engine came to life. She caught a glimpse of Kavello's contorted features before the inside light winked out and the car peeled away. She raced after it, squinting and trying to make out the license plate.

Darcy bounded into the street. He stopped directly in the path of the car.

"Move," she screamed at him.

The car swerved to avoid him, catching the side of a parked vehicle before accelerating down the street. Jordan reached Darcy's side and both watched the tail lights vanish.

Her feet hurt like hell. She snapped at Darcy. "What was that stunt? If he hadn't turned his wheel at the last second, you'd be dead."

"Well, pet, it's human nature to swerve when something jumps into your path. I was hoping he'd pile up good."

Residents rushed out to investigate the cause of the ruckus. One man combined inconsolable curses with strings of dire threats. Undoubtedly, the owner of the damaged vehicle.

Darcy turned back to the apartment building. "Let's talk to Kelsi and see what's going on. First, I'm going to call the cops."

Kelsi sprawled on an ugly, green couch, drinking directly from a bottle of red wine. "Did you catch him?"

Jordan sat beside her, leaping up as a spring poked her ass. "He got away. What do you think he was looking for?"

"Don't know. He asked if my roommate, Sherryn Groves, was here earlier tonight. When I told him I just got home, he went shit-crazy."

Darcy overheard her comment and said to the cop on the phone, "Wait one sec, please."

He addressed Kelsi, "Did you say Groves? Spell her first name."

Kelsi did so.

"Okay, and how do you know the name of the intruder?"

"He's in our Death's Reality course. He must be the guy Sherryn's secretly dating. He seemed surprised when I answered the door. Guess Sherryn never told him we were roommates."

Darcy's eyes took on the colour of ice under an Arctic sun. "Just to be clear. You, Sherryn Groves, and Jag Kavello are students of Professor Stride?"

Kelsi nodded. "His real name is Jared, but he doesn't like anyone to call him that."

"Now there's a link worth pursuing," Jordan interjected, touching the slight swelling on her temple. She better clean the abrasion with disinfectant in case the skin was broken. Fucking toilet plunger.

Darcy spoke into his phone again. "Okay, the suspect's name is Jared Kavello. Yes. Forcible entry and assault. You're welcome."

Darcy asked, "What happened when you told him you hadn't seen Sherryn tonight?"

Kelsi licked the wine droplets from her lips and frowned at the bottle. "He stuck his foot in the door, called me a liar, and slapped me across the face. Then he dragged me into the kitchen and rummaged through the drawers until he found the tape."

Jordan removed the wine bottle from Kelsi's grip and handed her a glass of water. "And?" she encouraged her to continue.

"He asked me where she lived in Ottawa and what her mother's name was. I lied and said I didn't know. He kept ranting that she had his money. I think he's gone nuts. He taped my mouth and started to trash the apartment after threatening to beat the shit out of me. When he heard you knock, he ran for the bathroom."

"How did you manage to call Darcy?"

"My phone was in my back pocket. I got a finger on it and tried to hit 911 while Jag was ransacking the drawers. But, I couldn't tell whether the phone was right side up. I programmed Mr. P in as number one, and I guess I hit that a bunch of times."

Jordan left Kelsi slumped on the couch and joined Darcy in the kitchen where he was completing a call, speaking in French too rapidly for her to comprehend. When he disconnected, she asked, "And where the hell is Emergency Response?"

"On their way. An Alert has been circulated for his 2009 grey Ford Taurus with damage to the front right bumper. I talked to *Tante* Dot. When I mentioned Groves and Kavello, with a connection to Lucas Stride, she said she was sending over a detective sergeant with knowledge of the case."

He called out to Kelsi. "What's the make, model, and colour of Sherryn's vehicle? If you have the plate number, that would be super."

To Jordan, he added, "I'm concerned about Sherryn. The sooner we find her, the better."

Kelsi responded, "She drives a white Forester, Subaru, a couple of years old. I don't know the license plate number. Do you think Sherryn's in trouble?"

Jordan headed for the door. "There's a white Subaru in the parking lot."

CHAPTER TWENTY-ONE

Friday, 11:00 p.m.

THE AMBULANCE TRANSPORTED SHERRYN TO THE NEAREST hospital. Kelsi accompanied her friend, promising Darcy that she would contact Sherryn's mother.

An authoritative voice reached out of the clutch of Ident Officers crowding the hallway outside the apartment.

"Monsieur Piermont. What is going on here, and how are you involved?"

Darcy started. "*Bonjour*, Detective Sergeant Perrot. Always good to see you. Only wish it were under more pleasant circumstances."

"That wouldn't be your black Acura parked on the sidewalk in front of this building, would it?"

"Ah, now, Nicoline. We were in a hurry. My new assistant, Kelsi Chong, was in a bit of a quandary, and we had no time to lose."

The petite woman snorted, sounding very much like Jordan. Did they teach that derisive sound at police colleges? Darcy didn't have to look at Jordan to know her eyes had narrowed to slits.

He cleared his throat and introduced the women — in English —

citing names, ranks and respective police services. They nodded civilly to each other.

"Nicoline and I met during a case, a few years ago, when she was with the Montréal police," he said to Jordan.

"And, you are Darcy's current *amour*, Jordan?" Nicoline asked courteously.

"Yup. Current. That's me. You're the ex, I take it?" Jordan responded.

"*Oui*. One of many. The stories I could tell you. Perhaps you and I can have lunch one day?"

An unspoken signal seemed to pass between the two women. The corners of Jordan's lips quirked up, and Nicoline winked. Both appeared amused by Darcy's discomfort.

Darcy broke into the conversation. "I take it my aunt contacted you after I called her about tonight's events."

"*Oui*. Deputy Director Dufresne is aware I responded to a crime scene at the city morgue this evening. When you mentioned the names Sherryn Groves and Jared Kavello in connection with a home invasion and assault, we initiated a search for Kavello. Ms. Groves came to our station this afternoon, before the discovery of Professor Stride's body. She revealed a crime of fraud and extortion by Mr. Kavello. She confessed to playing a part in the second charge. Apparently, Kavello defrauded Ms. Groves' parents of their investments some time ago, and she followed him here to Québec City hoping to find proof of his crime." Nicoline's eyes rolled, a testament to her opinion on the attempts of amateurs seeking justice.

She touched Darcy's shoulder. "There may have been a slight language problem during the interview. I am not clear how Ms. Groves knew where to find Kavello. The alleged crime against her parents took place in Ottawa. Ms. Groves was attending McGill University in Montréal at the time."

"I think I may be the missing link," Darcy conceded. "Sherryn was one of my last clients in Montréal before I moved here. She knew the name of the investment broker who had defrauded her parents. He fled the area, and she hired me to locate him. I did so and gave her his address in Québec City." He decided not to mention that his aunt and the professor were long-time acquaintances. That was up to his aunt to disclose.

Nicoline's cool eyes appraised Darcy's features. "We found a partial fingerprint on the belt buckle of the victim at the morgue, as well as some tissue particles under the fingernails. The victim had a ski mask in his pocket. Whether it belonged to him or his assailant, we don't yet know. We have no prints or DNA on file for Kavello, so we must apprehend him to obtain a sample. If we get a match on either, then *voila*, we have found our man."

"Do you need my help?" Darcy asked.

"How about making sure I don't trip over you during my investigation?"

"Fair enough," Darcy agreed.

He waited while Jordan and Nicoline exchanged business cards, then led the way outside to his vehicle where, *naturellement*, a parking violation ticket rested under his wiper blade.

Jordan climbed barefoot into the passenger seat, tossing her shoes on the floor. "So, Nicoline is one of your former snuggle bunnies? Just one of many?"

"Now, don't say it like that. Please never let her hear the term snuggle bunny. Besides, it was a long time ago."

"Before or after your quickie Las Vegas marriage and quicker divorce?"

Darcy gave her a side glance. "You don't forget anything, do you? Me, I feel a sudden case of amnesia coming on."

CHAPTER TWENTY-TWO

Saturday, 1:00 a.m.

JORDAN DOZED IN THE SEAT BESIDE DARCY AS HE DROVE TO HIS CONDO in Upper Town. Once in a while she twitched and uttered little sounds of distress. He reached over and squeezed her hand in case she fought demons in her sleep.

With his urging, she revived long enough to stumble up the stairs to the bedroom. She flung herself across the bed and fell back to sleep. The bottoms of her feet were dirty and cut. Darcy wiped them with wet towels, then sprayed antiseptic on the scratches. Now, what to do about that dress? It had taken her ten minutes to wiggle into it.

By the time Darcy peeled the dress off and tucked Jordan between the sheets, he was numb with exhaustion. He undressed and slid in beside her, manoeuvering his body against hers and wrapping his arms around her.

———

When he opened his eyes, sunlight flooded in through the open drapes.

The shower was running. He rolled over and waited until it stopped. Jordan bounded from the bathroom, dressed in olive green shorts and a yellow tank top. Her damp hair sprinkled droplets of water over Darcy's chest as she sank onto the edge of the bed.

"Let's go, Piermont. You promised me one more day of sight-seeing. Move it. It's almost 9 o'clock."

Darcy groaned. "Why are you so cheery in the morning? It's unnatural."

"I'm not, usually. I'm on holiday and I've a lot to see yet."

"Are you sure you don't want to jump back in here with me for an hour or so?"

"Well, aren't you the optimist? But, no, you can take me someplace special for breakfast, then I want to visit a few art galleries. I'll make coffee while you shower."

"But, your feet ..." he protested. No use. Jordan was already half way down the stairs.

In the kitchen, she handed him a cup of coffee strong enough to shrivel his tongue.

Jordan said, "I called the hospital about Sherryn, but they wouldn't tell me anything. You should contact Kelsi. She might have some news from Sherryn's mother."

Darcy added a healthy dollop of cream to his cup and called Kelsi's cell. While he listened to her update, he watched Jordan shove her feet into Puma walking shoes with nary a flinch. Warrior indeed. But, was she really his warrior queen? Nicoline's entrance into the scene last night had thrown him into a near panic. It hadn't been a serious relationship, and he would do his best to assure Jordan of this.

"Sherryn's recovery will be slow but steady," he told Jordan with relief. "She has a concussion, several broken ribs, an assortment of bruises, and needed stitches in her lip. Kelsi says the doctors expect she'll be released to her mother's care in a few days."

"That's good news. I hope your ex-girlfriend has posted a guard outside her hospital room until Kavello is in custody."

"From God's ear to your lips, my pet," Darcy answered, earning him a quizzical look from Jordan. That phrase may not have translated well from the French in his head. "Let's get you some food. I'm taking you to Le Lapin Sauté in Lower Town."

"Doesn't that mean fried rabbit?"

"More or less," Darcy said. She understood more French than she let on.

"Lead on, MacSnoop."

They took the Funiculaire, a glass-walled railway car that descended almost 200 feet over the ramparts to Lower Town.

Jordan was delighted by the ride and glimpses into the décor of condos nestled into the embankment. When the car settled, they made their way through a convenience store to rue du Petit-Champlain.

After breakfast, they looked at the offerings of street artists and browsed galleries and bookstores. Jordan didn't buy anything, but she was tireless in her intent to see it all.

They stopped for lunch at the Il Bello restaurant and ordered fresh egg pasta with a basil tomato sauce over slow-braised beef, splitting a bottle of Pian di Rèmole.

———

When they returned to the condo in late afternoon, Darcy complained he couldn't swallow another bite for at least three days.

"I don't remember these many steps," Jordan confessed as Darcy steadied her.

"That's probably because you're seeing double," he teased.

She swayed slightly on her way into the kitchen. "I need caffeine."

"Again? I mean, that should hit the spot. I'll check my office phone for messages, while you make coffee. Later, maybe we'll have a lie-down together?"

She called to him from the kitchen. "I saw some art pieces today that I would buy if I won the lottery. I'm ashamed to admit I live in a city of 125 galleries and have yet to visit any of them."

He waited until she joined him. "So, you think I'm a good influence on you?" He pulled her down beside him on the couch.

"Maybe, in the art department." She reached up to mess his hair. He blocked her move, grabbed her wrist, and left a trail of kisses to the bend of her elbow. She used her free hand to rub the top of his head. "But the levels of depravity you've dragged me to in other areas, cancels one positive influence."

"I've tried my best," Darcy responded, modestly.

She stretched out on the couch with her feet on his lap. "Monday, when I'm fighting traffic on Yonge Street, I'm going to remember this time with you. The river cruise, the mountains in the distance, Montmorency Falls you insist are higher than Niagara, the fabulous churches and buildings older than our country. And someday, I'd like to spend a night at the Château Frontenac."

"Consider it done. Next visit, I'll book us there for a couple of nights."

"Let's take one visit at a time."

"We'll do it your way, but I'm going to miss waking up with you beside me."

They were both silent for a few moments before Darcy said, "I want to see more of you, not less. What do you say about that?"

"I feel the same, but who knows what the future holds? Long distance relationships are hard to maintain.

"Not if we're determined to make it work."

"Come on, Darcy. You just moved your business here from Montréal. I'm six years in with the Toronto Police Service. My life is there, yours is here."

"I don't suppose you'd consider transferring to the Québec City Police?"

She laughed, not in a humorous way. "You know I'd have to be fluent in French to get a job on the same force as your ex-girlfriend, Nicoline."

"Perhaps Piermont Investigations will open an office in Toronto. My cousin, Pierre-Claude, may be willing to take over this location."

"Slow the hell down. How about you come visit me in October for Thanksgiving? My family celebrates at our cottage on Sparrow Lake. I'll introduce you to the great outdoors."

"If I'm roughing it, I'll need lots of cuddling. All this talk about nature has made me long for a nap. Interested?"

"Lead on, you tattooed hunk of man-love. Shit, will you listen to me, I might be a wee bit trashed."

CHAPTER TWENTY-THREE

Sunday, 2:00 p.m.

JAG SLUMPED ON A BENCH ON RUE DES PARLEMENTAIRES. DESPITE THE late August heat, he kept his sweatshirt zipped to hide the blood-spattered T-shirt.

By now the cops would have an Alert out for him. He'd ditched the Taurus in a wooded area outside the city. Sleeping in the park for two nights sucked. He stunk and his teeth were coated with a layer of grunge.

If he had a gun, he'd go postal. Except, he'd run out of bullets trying to eliminate all the people who had fucked up his brilliant plan. Hands down, the first bullet would go to Sherryn, the bitch who screwed him over. Alive, she was one more witness to take him down. Then there were those nut jobs in Sherryn's apartment. Who the hell were they? The bitch was strong and nearly caught him going out the window, and the guy threw himself in front of his car. He wished he had run over him.

It didn't even matter whether Sherryn was alive or dead. Too many other people had seen his face. He should have offed the roommate while he was there.

Jag checked his phone for the time. He should be halfway to the

Caymans by now, but the airport would be crawling with cops. How had everything got so fucked up?

He had chosen Québec City as a temporary haven. Thanks to Sherryn, he couldn't use his credit cards or passport, couldn't even go back to his apartment to grab some clothes or the small stash of money hidden in a plastic bag in the toilet tank. He checked his wallet. A hundred and fifty-seven dollars and change. Enough money for gas.

Jag bought junk food at a convenience store, then surveyed the street for a new set of wheels to get to Toronto as quickly as possible. He could disappear there for now. His first stop would be a bank to access his offshore account. With the cash, he'd purchase a new identity and a passport.

Jag spotted a cherry-red Ferrari parked at the curb. Same colour as his Jaguar. Hands in his pockets, he sauntered over.

Squatting behind the front passenger wheel, he reached under and groped. Nothing here. He strolled to the other side and repeated the action. This time, his fingers found a magnetized, metal box. He pulled it free. The dumbass didn't deserve to own this beauty. He removed the key fob from the box, released the door lock, and slid onto the leather bucket seat.

Exhaustion gave way to exhilaration as he eased the Ferrari into traffic. The rumble of the V8 fed his high. He fought the urge to jam his foot onto the gas pedal.

He needed to access Hwy. 73, cross the Pierre Laporte Bridge to the south shore of the St. Lawrence, then pick up Autoroute 20. The A-20 turned into the 401 at the Ontario border and, from there, clear sailing to Toronto.

The traffic thinned on rue de la Promenade. He surrendered to his speed addiction.

His euphoria nose-dived when he spotted a cop car shoot out of a side street and fish-tail into the lane behind him.

He increased his speed to 120 kilometres per hour, then 160. Checking the rear-view mirror again, he laughed out loud at the cop trying to keep up with him. Then, another cruiser joined the pursuit, siren wailing.

"Welcome to the party, assholes." No way would they chance a high-speed chase within city limits.

Flashing lights at a railway crossing drew his attention. A locomotive sped toward him. He rammed the accelerator to the floor. The Ferrari's front end cleared the track. The train smashed into the rear quarter panel, flipping the car into the air, and slamming it against a hydro pole.

The carbon body crumbled around Jag. He opened his mouth to scream. The gas tank ruptured then exploded, entombing him in a ball of flames.

CHAPTER TWENTY-FOUR

Sunday, 6:00 p.m.

DARCY AND JORDAN RAN AT THE AUTOMATIC DOOR OF THE airport, and it slid open just in time. With Jordan's suitcase flying behind him, he grabbed her hand and pulled her towards the check-in counter.

Jordan protested, "We should have left sooner."

"Who was it who couldn't find her passport?" Darcy muttered. More loudly, he said, "I've upgraded your ticket to first-class. Let's pretend I forgot to tell you."

"Well, thanks. But, you shouldn't have done that. I'm okay in vermin class."

"Not for my queen." There hadn't been another airline flying from Québec City to Toronto today, so a ticket change was the best he could do. With any luck, the attendants wouldn't be the same as when she flew in.

"Lots of cops here today," she commented. "They must be watching for Kavello. I'll look out for him on the flight in case he slipped through and is heading west."

Darcy shook off the image of Jordan engaged in hand-to-hand

confrontation with a desperate killer at 37,000 feet. In first class, yet. He knew who he'd put his money on. "You just sit back and relax on the flight, luv. Have a glass of champagne. Kavello won't get through this cordon of officers."

His cell buzzed. "Nicoline. I'd better take this." He avoided eye contact with Jordan.

"Bonjour. What can I do for you?" After a moment's listening, Darcy interjected, "Why isn't the DNA result a priority anymore?"

When he ended the call, Jordan said, "Spit it out. I'm short on time."

"Kavello tried to outrun the cops in a stolen Ferrari. Then, he tried to outrun a train. The train won. Bloody good riddance, I'd say."

"Karma's a bitch. Sherryn and Kelsi can quit looking over their shoulders now. Take care of your aunt. I know she's devastated by Lucas's death. Anyway, bye, Piermont, it's been a blast." Jordan gave him a quick kiss on the lips and was gone from his sight.

———

He drove home with a heavy heart and wandered into his office. He poured himself an inch of single malt whiskey and dropped into his chair. Back to work tomorrow. Kelsi would be in, chatting his ear off, full of news about Sherryn and her own harrowing experience. Thankfully, he and Jordan arrived at her apartment when they did.

He swirled the amber liquid in the glass, sniffed it, and put it down. Not really his drink of choice. The decanter of Glenfiddich in the office was kept only to impress clients. It reminded him of the empty bottle of whiskey he and Jordon found in Professor Stride's suite at the Frontenac. What a shame — a man who spent his life sharing his knowledge died at the hands of a useless shit like Kavello.

Darcy picked up his glass. "You won't be forgotten, Lucas." He downed the whiskey in one gulp, shuddering when the fire hit his stomach. "Blimey!"

CHAPTER TWENTY-FIVE

Several weeks later

ELEVEN SHIFTS. JORDAN LIFTED HER FOOT ONTO THE BENCH IN the locker room and tied her shoe. She pressed her forehead to her raised knee and closed her eyes. She wasn't sure she could stay awake to drive home. She better leave her car at the station and take a taxi. On second thought, that would mean a trip back tomorrow to get it.

The door to the corridor opened and a male voice shouted. "Blair! You in there?"

"Here," Jordan acknowledged. Now what?

"Asherby wants you in his office. ASAP."

Jordan climbed two floors to Staff-Sergeant Asherby's lair and rapped on the door. She ran through tonight's raid in her mind. No injuries, including three Tong gang members picked up in the act of transferring bundles of automatic rifles and heroin from shipping containers to the back of a van. The squad was pissed they didn't nab a few kingpins along with the soldiers, but some days you take what you can get.

A voice rumbled for her to enter. "Pull up a seat, Blair."

Whatever it was, Asherby didn't look pleased.

"I stayed late to tell you about a new development. I should be in bed with my wife."

"I'm sure she'll understand, sir." Jordan hoped this was true, for Asherby's sake. He was on his third wife.

His frown deepened. "You've been seconded to a new inter-provincial task force, effective Monday."

"Inter-provincial, sir? Wouldn't the Ontario Provincial Police be leading this?" Where was this going? Was someone on her squad trying to get rid of her?

"The OPP thinks they're in charge of everything. In this case, they're working a joint operation with the Québec provincials. Due to the resurgence of outlaw biker activity in Toronto and Québec City, this new task force requires bodies from the Toronto Service and the Québec City Service. Are you keeping count, Blair? That's four police jurisdictions. Five, after the Mounties climb aboard the fuckmobile and take the wheel."

A three-level operation: federal, provincial, and municipal. Jordan's mouth went dry. "But, why me, sir? I don't ..."

"Hold on. This is shaping up to be a turf war of the ugliest kind. And, that's before the bikers get involved. You and two other Toronto officers will be joining the team of Operation Fat Boy, God help you. Your initial assignment will be in Québec City."

"I don't speak French, sir. Will I be undercover?"

"I don't believe so, Blair."

"Then, what's my role?"

Asherby flipped open a folder, then slammed it shut again. "Haven't a clue and kinda don't care. I assume it's because of your work with gangs and arms dealing. I can't afford to lose you, but nobody cares what I want. Deputy Chief Dolan's office asked for you specifically."

"I never met him."

Asherby opened the folder again and dug deeper. "Request came from Deputy Director Dufresne in Québec City. Know him?"

She choked out her response. "She's a woman. I met her once."

"You must have made quite an impression. Good or bad, remains to be seen. You have a nine o'clock meeting Monday morning in Deputy

Chief Dolan's office. He'll brief you and the other seconded officers. You're dismissed."

Jordan stopped at the door. "Do you know how long the assignment will last? When can I rejoin my squad?"

For the first time, Asherby met her gaze. "I'd say you're looking at a couple of years on the task force. We can't hold your current job that long. When you get back, we'll slot you in somewhere else until a space opens up in Guns and Gangs. If that's what you still want."

"Thank you, sir."

"Good luck, Blair. I suggest you sign yourself up for some French lessons."

Jordan pushed through the stairwell door and sank down on the top step. She'd have to sub-lease her condo. And put her belongings in storage. Tears sprang from her eyes and she swiped her sleeve across her face. Wouldn't do to be caught bawling like a fucking toddler.

Her hand shook so violently, she had difficulty pulling her cell out. It was the middle of the night. Good.

A sleep-congested voice answered. "*Allô*? Jordan? Is everything alright ..."

"Piermont! Talked to Auntie Dot lately? Have you heard of Operation Fat Boy?"

"Uh, *mon petit chou*, Auntie is fine, and the only fat boy I know is a Harley motorcycle model."

"Fair warning. I'm going to kill you. Painfully and creatively."

"A wee bit harsh, luv. What did I do?"

"Like you don't know. When I'm done with you, your family won't find enough parts to turn you into stained-glass windows or tattoo ink. I'm coming for you, Piermont."

AUTHORS' NOTE AND ACKNOWLEDGEMENTS

Thanks for reading *Death's Footprint*. We hope you enjoyed book #2 in our Blair and Piermont crime fiction series. If you did, please post your comments on Amazon or wherever you purchased the book.

———

Special thanks to D.L. Houghton who critiqued our manuscript and provided valuable input. We're grateful for on-going encouragement from members of our Genre5 Authors: Elizabeth Lindsay, Pamela Blance, and D.L. Houghton.

To our beta readers, our sincere appreciation for your comments: Lara Inneo, Maureen Langford, and Scott Houghton.

We have Cheryl R. Cowtan to thank for designing the cover for Death's Footprint and sharing marketing tips.

Thank you to Marie-Claude Brousseau, the Director of Public Relations at the Fairmont Château Frontenac for a guided tour during our stay at this historic, world-renowned hotel.

ABOUT THE AUTHORS

Donna's novella, *Targeted*, published Nov. 2015, is book #1 in the Blair and Piermont crime thriller series. It's set in the Caribbean on Roatán Island, Honduras. Book #2, *Death's Footprint*, published Apr. 2017, takes place in Canada's historic Québec City. Both *Targeted* and *Death's Footprint* are co-authored with award winning mystery author, Gloria Ferris.

Before joining the fiction writing industry, first as a freelance editor and then as a published author, Donna was communication manager for the Canadian Network of Toxicology Centres. Prior to that, she tutored ESL students; taught college-level education courses for ten years; and founded a registered private vocational school.

A keen cottager, Donna enjoys the challenges of climbing in and out of her kayak without getting dunked and trying to outsmart fish. Home is a country property on the outskirts of Guelph, Ontario. She is a member of International Thriller Writers and the Crime Writers of Canada.

www.donnawarnerauthor.com
www.djwarnerconsulting.blogspot.ca
Author's Page on Amazon.com: http://tinyurl.com/o9votoo
Contact me at donnawarnerauthor@gmail.com

Gloria Ferris is the award-winning author of the Cornwall & Redfern mysteries that feature serious crimes and far-from-serious protagonists. *Death's Footprint* is her second crime thriller, quick read, co-written with author, Donna Warner.

When not writing, Gloria works on character profiles, researches plotlines, reads everything, and is often heard to mutter, "I wish I'd written that!" She is a member of the Crime Writers of Canada, the International Thriller Writers, and the Alliance of Independent Authors. Gloria returned to her native Guelph, Ontario, after retiring from her job as procedure writer at a nuclear power plant. She spent more than twenty-five years in Kincardine and Port Elgin, small towns which inspire her mysteries.

www.gloriaferris.com
Visit Gloria's author page on Amazon.com: http://tinyurl.com/lx62765
Contact me at gloriaferris@yahoo.ca